Jim Bostjancic

THE SWEETEST DAYS

Limited Special Edition. No. 15 of 25 Paperbacks

Jim Bostjancic is a screen and television series writer from Canada. This debut work of fiction is based on one of his unproduced screenplays.

To veterans unable to find a place…

Jim Bostjancic

THE SWEETEST DAYS

AUSTIN MACAULEY PUBLISHERS™
LONDON • CAMBRIDGE • NEW YORK • SHARJAH

Copyright © Jim Bostjancic (2020)

The right of Jim Bostjancic to be identified as author of this work has been asserted by him in accordance with section 77 and 78 of the Copyright, Designs and Patents Act 1988.

All rights reserved. No part of this publication may be reproduced, stored in a retrieval system, or transmitted in any form or by any means, electronic, mechanical, photocopying, recording, or otherwise, without the prior permission of the publishers.

Any person who commits any unauthorised act in relation to this publication may be liable to criminal prosecution and civil claims for damages.

This is a work of fiction. Names, characters, businesses, places, events, locales, and incidents are either the products of the author's imagination or used in a fictitious manner. Any resemblance to actual persons, living or dead, or actual events is purely coincidental.

A CIP catalogue record for this title is available from the British Library.

ISBN 9781528930727 (Paperback)
ISBN 9781528930734 (Hardback)
ISBN 9781528966405 (ePub e-book)

www.austinmacauley.com

First Published (2020)
Austin Macauley Publishers Ltd
25 Canada Square
Canary Wharf
London
E14 5LQ

Chapter 1

A Buddhist monk in Montreal for an ecumenical symposium was in a cab stopped at the foot of Autoroute Ville Marie expressway when he saw someone touched by heaven. The man had a crooked back and was dressed in a tattered suit.

Had a brief case in one hand and was licking a melting ice cream cone with such joy. Innocence, the Monk reflected. This was no osteoporosis, senior. He was a young man. Peter Pan boy.

Gary's stoop made him look 20 years older from far but close, his blonde hair and baby-face made him appear 10 years younger than his 32. He just polished off a coffee ice cream and was flying high on mocha sweetness.

Moments like these checked degrees of anxiety he experienced better than medication he was prescribed to what psychiatrists described as 'mental illness'.

The light changed, and the cab lurched forward.

The Monk glanced back at the slouched stranger in his reverie or little world, whatever crooked back standing on the sidewalk was feeling, that was Nirvana.

This was not the Sweetest Day. For one, Gary was borderline diabetic which checked him from eating sugar often. And two, since he was on social assistance, could not afford to but was treating himself to a sweet because he was on his way to applying for a job he felt he had an excellent chance getting.

10 minutes later he was standing on the corner in Montreal's Little Burgundy neighbourhood, among the row houses painted blue, green, indigo, and red. Residents in this enclave painted the brick exteriors of homes to mirror Montreal's rainbow of inclusion.

The proprietor of Mr. Bubble's Car Wash was a portly, Greek fellow in his fifties. Bushy eyebrows. Stained undershirt. Hairy back. He was nursing a cigarillo. Gary found the smoke stifling and coughed. Yet the aroma pleasant. Silently lipping to himself, the Greek reviewed Gary's application for employment.

"You're from English Canada? Served in Afghanistan?"

"With Canadian forces," Gary concurred.

"And your best job since being back is selling ice cream in Winnipeg?"

Gary nodded. Mr. Bubbles, or the Greek, looked at Gary. Suspicious more than confused now.

"Why?"

Gary hesitated. Should he tell him or not?

He decided to be honest. Maybe a Mr. Bubbles kind of guy would understand?

"Panic attacks," Garry added.

"Panic attacks? What do you mean by that?"

A pang of insecurity befell Gary causing him to hesitate.

If he explained. Was honest, might still win.

"Sometimes when things go on I get very scared. And my heart beats very fast. And it feels like I'm going to die."

Now that threw the Greek a loop.

What in frigging, damn hell, he thought.

A Montreal Urban Community garbage truck pulled up.

"Go Green' painted on the sides in French.

There was no concealing Gary's stressed and pronounced obvious gasp as two strapping sanitation engineers emptied overflowing containers of trash in the rear of the truck.

"What?"

The Greek inquired, puzzled by Gary's reaction?

"Garbage men."

"So?"

"They better not be here to take me away."

"Take you away?"

He'd met his share of jailbirds and kooks searching for employment after being released from the slammer, but this

Gary guy and a former army war vet, on top of it, left him beyond baffled. This desperado is way too messed up.

"I don't know what kind of a head case you are, but I'm not going to be able to hire you, buddy."

And that was it. The opportunity was gone and replaced by something painful that imbued Gary. Not pain that physically hurt like being punched or kicked. An inner feeling of loss. Dread. Defeat. Death. Just like in Afghanistan. Like war buddies wiped out. His mom gone. Failure to thrive. Reasons he'd always moved on. Gary strode off. Moved pretty quick with pep. Not arrogant or insolent tough, but being ex-military still in shape.

A maelstrom of confusion consumed Gary now.

He stopped. Reached in his suit pocket and produced an envelope. He was only supposed to take these at night because they made him sleepy. He popped the little tablets into his mouth.

Medication designed to do battle and free him from the dudgeon of doom. He hoped it would work in time before he would have to face his social worker and explain the reason why he didn't get the job. She or the psychiatrists didn't know when he took tablets during the day, 99% of the time they didn't work.

The effects of the medication kicked in immediately.

He was getting drowsy. His eyelids got heavy.

He couldn't think. He had to hide so he could close his eyes and sleep somewhere safe. Forty minutes later the security man shook Gary who jumped—and snapped awake.

"No sleeping – out," the guard sneered in Quebecois French.

He tried to be polite but learned it was better being a rough dealing with bums who passed out where Concordia University students were supposed to be studying. At 60 it felt good intimidating ne'er-do-wells with the power of his voice.

Gary marched out pronto. He didn't have a clue what the security man said but could tell by his tone it was uninviting. Gary only understood a few words in French.

Moving to a city where he didn't speak the language was a good idea. If people said unkind things and you couldn't understand what they were saying, so it couldn't hurt.

Montreal. It was the perfect place to try again.

At De Maisonneuve and Guy Street his balance was off.

He was dizzy from untimely ingesting his medication.

The tablets knocked him out and he fell asleep while hiding. He caught a glimpse of a passing clock that read 5:15.

Dudgeon of doom feeling dissipated but his welfare worker was going to be angry because he was 2 hours late.

Lucky the office was only a few blocks from the metro.

The receptionist told Gary his social worker Ms. Jepsen left. He left a message that he'd been unable to obtain the job and the receptionist picked up the phone and spoke in French. Gary didn't understand what she said but sensed it was not good.

On the other end of the line, Gary's caseworker Ms. Genevieve Jepsen was furious. Fifty-six years old. An obese woman who always wore loose-fitting dresses to conceal her figure. Clients do not dictate or impose on her by being late and irresponsible in a system that was overwhelmed.

It was further exacerbated for having faith in him only to be proved wrong. Unlike so many of the other young people in their prime destroyed by mental illness, she believed Gary could rise above it.

She wanted to abandon Gary for failing her too.

Upon reconsidering, realised she did not have all the facts.

There was not enough love to go around in the world. She knew that personally. A spinster fraught with weight issues since adolescence. Men ignoring her. Never dating.

Single for years and alone.

Gary observed her while she re-read the notes in his file. Her obesity didn't register. *She was old,* he thought. Lots of wrinkles on her face. These lines were not from overexposure to sun or age but battle scars acquired over years fighting for Montreal's most neglected.

The vast majority losses. Some of those losses broke her heart. The reason why she even took on Gary's case file was because he was from Western Canada. Did not speak a word of French. A strike against him before he could even be helped. He had been her client for 2 months. Counselled him 30 minutes, twice a week. And he'd been in the hospital twice so far.

Notes indicated he had been discharged from the Canadian Forces. Deemed unfit for service. It was vague and inconclusive. *This is the Federal Government,* she thought. *Doing their fancy dancing.*

Passing the buck to provinces or municipalities to deal with the headache. She flipped to the next page of the file. Composite psychiatric evaluations followed him from Vancouver B.C. Eastbound. Calgary—borderline personality. Winnipeg—Bipolar disorder. Toronto—psychotic ideation. Ottawa—schizophrenic.

His collar was skewed otherwise he was clean. Neat. Always in a suit. No smoke stained fingers nor disregard of hygiene with respect to hair, teeth, or body cleanliness. It was evident Gary did not abuse alcohol or drugs like many others. Something was amiss. What was right about him was undocumented. Irrelevant? Unknown?

"Jarry…"

Like everyone else in the city, Ms. Jepson mispronounced his name. Instead of regular, 'Gary' it came out as 'Jarry' when Montrealers voiced it in their French, Quebecois accents.

"How are you feeling?" she began in broken English.

"Like a seesaw. Up and down," Gary answered.

"Good or bad?"

"Mostly good. A little bad," Gary added.

"Keeping busy?"

"Just like always. Looking for a job. Going for walks. Visiting the park."

"And life, Jarry?"

"Welfare gives me 300 dollars for rent. Eighty dollars for a Metrobus pass. Ten dollars for my cell phone. Ten dollars a day for food. And if I have anything left at the end, I visit Mount Royal Park on the Sweetest Day and go for a treat."

With the exception of unemployment, he seemed stable. When she probed further he couldn't mask the apprehension.

"Jarry, what happened at Mr. Bubbles?"

"I-I saw them again."

"Who?" she asked.

"The garbage men."

"You taking the medication?"

"It doesn't matter. They want to put me into the garbage bin and grind me up. They want me dead."

She wondered. What had he encountered in his life that made him reason in such a manner?

"In English, they call it 'delusion', Jarry. Mental illness."

"It's not. Feelings I get are real."

"Jarry… Feelings don't pay the rent. Feelings don't put food on the table."

"I can't."

"You can, Jarry."

"They ambushed my friends. I watched them die. Didn't do a damn thing."

"I'm sorry about the war, but you're back in Canada now."

"I'll try to be stronger next time."

"You can't try… you have to be, Jarry."

She looked at him. Refrained from disclosing certain information to him prior to applying for the job for concern it may burden him, but now she had no choice.

"Something I have to tell you."

"What?" Gary responded, agitated now.

"Government is making cuts. The city of Montreal is reducing welfare rates. It's going to have an effect. You won't be able to pay your rent."

A portal opened, and Gary was swallowed by the dudgeon of doom. He looked at her. Pleadingly. Pain. Despair. Defeat.

"Jarry? Jarry?"

It physically hurt. Doom. He couldn't speak.

She scribbled a number on a note pad. Handed it to him.

Gary looked at it and then back up at her.

"My mobile phone. You call me anytime you like."

She saw incipient tears in his big, puppy dog eyes now.
"Day or night?" Gary asked.
"Any time," she said softly.

Gary wandered around consumed by dread on downtown streets. He ended up on the 'Main' or St. Lawrence Boulevard and entered a cheap dollar store. Mindful of cuts to assistance, now, he could save money if he ate more pasta. Attempted to ask, but clerks were unable to communicate with him.

Grocery stores were frustrating when you didn't speak the official language. Paying cashiers announcing the bill in French when he didn't understand and searching for items when flyers and store aisle signs were not written in English was also discouraging.

The first thing he did arriving in any new city, Calgary, Winnipeg, Toronto, here, was searching for pals he'd serve with. He learned a buddy from Montreal died of wounds from a grenade. Encountered language barriers asking for directions, attempting to get his bearings looking up more acquaintances but could not track them and figured they moved on.

Arriving in August, his first response was thinking it was way warmer than Vancouver. While natives groaned over the humidity Gary thought, *Wow, it really feels like summer here.*

Not having funds and walking around in mild weather the frustration with the language transformed to awe when he became captivated by the names of city streets.

He played games trying to pronounce and whispering the romantic sounding roads to himself. 'Boulevard René-Lévesque. Gouin. Decarie. Eduard Mon Petite,' and the easy to say, 'Monkland,' which he found a laugh figuring this was where all the solo guys like him must live.

It made learning Montreal a joy compared to Vancouver and Calgary where most avenues and streets were numbered. There were no 'Pie-X. Lionel Groulx, Jean Talon, Avenue Du President De Kennedy or royal 'Queen Mary Roads', in Alberta or B.C.

Ms. Jepsen was boxed on the Jacques Cartier bridge during the commute home to the South Shore when she realised giving Gary 24-hour access to her personally breached protocol.

Why do I do this, she thought. She could not negate the defeated look on his face. Or did she do it because she was physically attracted to this lost man?

If she was slim and 20 years younger under these exact conditions and he threw himself in her arms and told her to save him she would say yes. Take him to her South Shore bungalow and no longer live a lonely life so they could be lovers.

The vehicle in front lurched a few feet then stopped.

This thinking was preposterous. He signed a form that enabled her to request information from the military to review their assessment and better understand him and was appraising a military psychiatrist on his progress. She was privy to more information about Gary than he knew and reflected on the promise he once had?

A fourth-floor bachelor apartment became vacant after a client had a psychotic break, murdered his girlfriend and then killed himself. She met Gary a few days prior to that. He arrived in town from Ottawa fleeing doctors telling him he was schizophrenic. He told her he didn't know the definition of schizophrenic but the word itself terrified him. When he was going to be detained under the mental health act, he pleaded he had not committed any crimes. A male psychiatric nurse attempted to restrain an agitated Gary, and a physical confrontation ensued.

Later, Gary saw police cars parked outside his rooming house and knew he had to run and hide. He used remaining welfare funds for food to buy a one-way bus ticket and escape 120 miles east to Montreal with just the clothes on his back.

Traffic came to a stop again. From a distance, she could make out the oval silhouette of the big 'O'. The apartment Jarry rented was near the Olympic stadium, the old home for the Montreal Expo's baseball franchise.

It was a working-class Francophone neighbourhood in transition with sporadic street crime and drug problems. The

Provincial government contributed a portion of expenses to Montreal social services for rent.

The landlord was amenable to homeless clients with mental health challenges whom case workers considered had the best chance of taking charge of their lives.

Gary was given the opportunity to fill out an application to reside there. It was up to the landlord to make a decision whom he best felt most comfortable with.

The time allocation of six months was prematurely up due to provincial budgetary cuts. Jarry did not have a job to compensate for the difference in order to remain.

Chapter 2

Felicity was 29 years old. Stunning. Blatantly beautiful. One hundred percent Nordic features that belied her French Canadian and Ukrainian roots. Bone structure sculpted face. Perfect symmetrical teeth. A smile that floored them and innocent dreamboat eyes that reeled the boys in. And from behind, her thick blonde hair flowing in the wind, long legs players fantasied wrapped around them, and sleek, New York Model Amazonian frame, literally caused fender benders when sashaying along St. Catherine Street in the summer. It also evinced malicious hatred.

Fellow females loathed Felicity for outshining them and coveted to be blessed with her surface attributes. The spotlight and the attention it commanded left her with few close friends to confide in. Yet Felicity was self-conscious of her body. Lithe and flexible but she felt gangly and thought she had more of a guy's build instead of the curves in the right places.

Her saving grace was she was not competitive in the go-getter ways of the world. Lacked competitive edge and mean streak. Deep down was simple as an elementary school girl. With only one personal focus and ambition in life. Shine bright down the road to becoming a ballerina star. Knew she was pretty but clueless of how profoundly striking she was to most men.

Years of training under world-renowned, Russian ex-patriot Olympian Gymnast Dancer Hanna Burnbaum left Felicity in dynamic physical condition.

Felicity worked part-time at Outremont dance school to earn enough money to go out clubbing with her few female friends and do some occasional shop therapy, but hardly enough to sustain herself in order to leave the family home she grew up in. One of these days she was going to make it. Star with a company and travel the world. Buy her own place. Earn the income to be independent.

"Twist. Turn. Hold. Smile. Posture. Superb," she enunciated in French to the group of 6-year-old girls training while their parents stood watch, beaming with pride.

"Congratulations on advancing to the next level,"

Felicity added in English while parents applauded their little princesses on.

Felicity was distracted today because a friend was getting married. There would be lots of single men from the groom's side attending. Maybe she would meet a cute guy?

Find her Mr. Perfect? Being as lovely and non-judgemental as she was, Felicity had encountered bizarre behaviour from numerous gentlemen callers with crushes on her since high school.

Everyone physically different in build, ethnicity, and temperament. Mama's boys—bumbling. Stumbling. Stuttering. Lonely boys drawn to her, stricken with fear they could barely look her in the face.

High tech geeks flummoxed by flirtatious signals sent she was interested. Players driven by erections that had to be fought off when they refused to take no for an answer. Bad boys with big muscles and tattoos driven by uncontrollable libidos that had to be fended off too.

Men were either dumb or an enigma. Or was it her?

What could be so difficult about love? Was it just a fairy tale? Did it even exist? Her imagination and the notion of romance. Just a disappointment. She was almost 30 years old. It never came.

People told her she was too pretty or too picky. Sure it was better if the guy looked good, but the truth was it didn't really matter what he looked like.

The only condition to Mr. Perfect is she had to be swept away by magic, because Felicity felt love was sacred. Where did this unrealistic expectation lead? Desperate enough to cry herself to slumber while listening to sweet love songs at night with earphones on in her bed. The world would never know this. How could they know it? To look upon Felicity, the embodiment of femininity and beauty. But the truth behind the exterior of awe the world beheld her and how she really felt inside, empty and achingly alone, was impossible for anyone to relate to.

Felicity considered Nancy her best friend. Along with a diploma from La Salle college in bookkeeping, Nancy worked full-time at the Outremont Ballet academy doing creative accounting and teaching dance when Felicity or Hanna were indisposed. She too trained years to be a professional but dropped out when she became pregnant and married.

Nancy became disillusioned with love when she caught her hubby in the sack with a hussy he worked with. Now she was divorced. Her heart had healed and she no longer believed in fairy tale romance like Felicity.

She distrusted men referring to them as 'subhumans'.

Swore if she ever met a worthy of male again, he'd have to jump through a hundred hoops to prove he was the exception. The dreams Nancy encouraged now were cheers for Outremont Ballet academy's little starlets and in raising and championing her 8-year-old son Joshua to be anything like his loser father she got hoodwinked into marrying.

Judy was Nancy's old roommate. Like Felicity she was physically striking, looking for everlasting love or her white knight in shining armour, but also open to sexy 'Mr. Tonights'.

The reception was in full swing and 3 guests of the groom were grinning over. They were 'hot' but none of what Judy called the 'dense hunks' had approached or asked them to dance. Deny, Henri, and Remi were Quebecois in their late 20s decked in identical white tuxedos.

"The stooges must have got a deal on the monkey suits," Nancy quipped.

Felicity and Judy laughed. Out of earshot, they grinned back. They were cousins who went to high school with the groom up in Chicoutimi and came down to Montreal to party. Their attention was concentrated on the knockout, Felicity.

"Get a load of her," commented Denis in Quebecois brogue.

"She is gorgeous," added Henri.

"I dare you to ask her to dance," added Remi.

"No way," Denis answered.

"Henri?"

"Never," he shot back.

"We men or mouses?" Denis asked.

It was an open bar. Denis returned with a whole bottle of Crown Royal. The bride's family was loaded, and guests were taking full advantage of it. Instead of nursing it slowly like they would have if issued tickets for a limited number of drinks, they swigged it down with gusto in gulps.

"What about now," Remi said.

"Too soon to tell," Denis added.

"I'm going to need more," Henri replied.

"We won't be able to stand," added Remi.

"Or dance," Dennis said.

"What ta' hell!" Henri declared.

"Salud," they announced in unison.

Down the hatch the flowing Crown Royal went.

"More and I fall on my face," slurred Remi.

"Need all the liquid courage we can get," said Denis.

"You going for the Goddess?" Henri asked.

"Never have the guts," Remi replied.

"Not in a million years," Denis added.

Felicity sat quietly while Remi and Henri babbled with Judy and Nancy for half an hour. Between, the hunks kept glancing and staring at her, then looking away, never saying 'boo' or a word to her.

Why? No way could they be so damn dumb or chicken, she thought. Judy and Nancy were getting so smashed by the endless flow from the open bar it didn't even register.

"*Love, look what you've done to me. Never thought I'd fall again so easily... ohhhhh, love.*" Written by David Foster and Willliam R. Ray Scaggs.

One of Felicity's favourite songs. Was from way before her time. The singer Boz Scaggs. 1976. Her daddy played the album on his ancient Yamaha turntable and introduced Felicity to lots of sweet songs from the '70s from another group called "Chicago."

After the slow danced song faded, Judy was necking with Remi in the corner. Henri was telling Nancy she was pretty and complimenting her she had nice hair.

It was that time of the month, and always made Felicity restless, so she practised and worked out more intensely to decompress. She had followed the calendar and this month her cycle was in sync with the full moon. When this happened, she felt hypersexual, emotionally vulnerable, and ultra-romantic. With the wedding, the solo feeling of exclusion was excruciating. Boz Scaggs cooing compounded the hurt, and she felt sickly down and depressed. I'm almost 30 years old.

Why is this happening? Why, she thought distraught, *do I always end up disappointed and alone?*

Nancy glanced back. She was unsure if Felicity was upset or unwell. They talked about the emotional rollercoaster and how frightening Felicity's experiences were during PMS.

She told Henri to hold his horses and proceeded to chat with Felicity for a sec.

"This always happens. Weddings. Parties. Social events," Felicity complained.

"They're not your type anyway," Nancy added.

Felicity was on the verge of tears now.

"It's literally been years since a single guy has even asked me to dance at a wedding."

"They're terrified of you."

"You're wrong."

"No, I'm not. They're intimidated.

"You're too perfect, Felicity."

"Players and geeks try to chat me up all the time."

It was true. Perverts or mama's boys seemed to be the only ones with gumption to approach her in clubs or on the street.

"The audition for 'the Nutcracker' is coming up. You'll meet a decent guy there," Nancy replied.

"99% of them will be gay," Felicity shot back.

Nancy sensed Felicity was unusually distraught, but when Henri sneaked up behind and scooped her up with a big smirk on his face, Nancy screamed in delight. When he put her down and told her how beautiful she was again, Nancy looked back over. Felicity knew it had been ages for Nancy. Hardly dating or having a guy appreciate her like this. She had no right to ruin it for her.

"Just go ahead!" Felicity said.

"You sure you're okay?"

Felicity considered it. What she was feeling was ugly and she was not well, but this did not entitle her to spoil her friend's evening.

"I'll deal with it! Have fun!"

Typically level-headed as Nancy was, she was so caught up in the moment looking at the lovable lunkhead Henri, grinning, she was unaware something was seriously wrong.

And Felicity's blessing was all she needed, so it didn't set off alarms it otherwise would.

"He's a whirlwind on the floor. Have a great time," Felicity added.

There really was something dangerously wrong. But there was no reason feeling horrible should prevent her best friend from feeling happy and loved.

"Call you tomorrow," Nancy yelled out as Henri carried her off like some Neanderthal over his shoulder. Felicity claimed her purse and jacket at coat check and promptly left.

Soon as Felicity exited the venue doors, she burst into tears.

She jumped in her grandmother's car and sped off.

She never cared much for drinking but was legally over the limit, and when a taxi cab overtook and cut in front of her without signalling, she screamed and slammed on the brakes. Pulled over and exploded into sobs. Something horrible seized her inside. Flipped a switch blinding her to reason and rationale.

"Mom, I want my mommy," she cried to herself.

Excruciating memories from when she was a little girl. Memories of her mother and what happened when they were last together. Years ago. When she was 4 years old.

She wailed. What is this, she searched her mind over and over. She could not consciously fight, deny, or control it. This was not her. Ten minutes later she arrived home still sobbing and feeling worse. It was if some malevolent entity gripped her innards and seized her mind now.

She clicked the garage door opener and drove in. Her father's pickup truck was gone, so he and her grandmother were out.

Whatever she drank unleashed something monstrous.

She had to stop this horror movie and knew precisely how to do so. Cognitive dissonance from her unconscious caused her to cry out: "NO!"

She was not in command of her faculties. Screamed again.

There was no one home to hear, save her, or call 911.

Internal dissonance ripping her apart. The solution a monstrosity. Infernal. An inconceivable self-destructive action.

With robot-like precision, Felicity grabbed the garden hose and placed it on the end on the exhaust. An absolutely perfect fit. A click and the garage door rolled down effortlessly too.

She placed the other end of the garden hose in the front seat of the car. Plopped down and rolled the window up.

At the edge of the garage, her Scottish Terrier dog Maxi was barking at her and whimpering while exhaust fumes began to overtake her. Her only mindset was to stop this feeling and to do that was to take decisive action. *I'll never find a boyfriend and be in love so this is it,* she thought.

*****

Even though this was a dishwasher's job, Gary knew he should have worn his suit. He always sported his suit when he applied for jobs. But the interview was at 8:00 p.m. He had dinner first and while eating pasta, spilled spaghetti sauce on his dress pants so had to wear a blue pullover sweater and grey slacks he received as a donation from the welfare office. This was to be trouble. It was going to hurt. But he would find out later it was also going to turn out good.

Gary was in the Greek restaurant on Du Park Avenue.

For 40 minutes he watched waitresses zip by balancing trays of shish-kebab while a house singer entertained patrons plucking a mandolin.

A waitress froze when she noticed Gary's expression. The weird thing was he was not irate but growing anxious from something she felt abnormal.

"He should have been back and told me to watch for you so I know he didn't forget," she said in Quebecois English twang.

"Non parlez vous French," Gary replied, flustered.

"No English."

No wonder. He looked too dapper for someone seeking a menial job even though the restaurant was the preeminent Greek establishment in the city, she thought.

"I'd text but left my phone by the bed to get here fast," Gary said.

The waitress extracted her personal mobile.

"One minute," she said and smiled.

"No, no, no, it's too late," Gary added stuttering.

She froze.

Gave Gary a puzzled look.

"Know the time," Gary added.

She held up the face of her phone. It read 8:46 p.m., saw the dread on Gary's face but was baffled as to why?

"I have to go now," Gary said.

"We're so busy…"

Gary split midsentence pronto – in fact fled.

*****

As he palmed the wheel of his cruiser taking corners fast, the constable's eyes scanned back and forth like in the movie 'RoboCop' searching for a white male suspect. Blonde hair, about 30, grey pants, blue sweater, who spoke English. The perpetrator just held up a grocery store with a hunting knife on Rue de la Gauchetière in Montreal's Chinatown.

Likely a meth addict, even though the description was of a well-dressed male, attire likely shoplifted from a department store on St. Catherine's street prior to the hold-up, the constable assumed.

Must be at least 8:47 Gary guessed as he sprinted down the side street in the Plateau Mont-Royal District, a neighbourhood he was disoriented in.

Realising he was heading east, instead of west towards the 'Main' or St. Lawrence Boulevard, when the constable spotted him. Suspect doesn't look like a hophead, but he's running? Why?

"Arret," the constable barked in French that came over the megaphone beside the red cheery lights on the rooftop of the police car. Gary instantly froze. Spotlight trained on him, looking like a deer in headlights.

"Don't move," he added, clearly enunciating in French.

The garbled tone of the constable's voice sent fear into Gary causing him to bolt. He didn't comprehend what this French,

Montreal policeman said, but he had to get to Mont-Royal Metro stop then switch subway lines to get to Pie-IX Boulevard, where he caught the bus for the short ride home in time to be safe.

The doors to the dudgeon of doom opened after 9 o'clock at night, and the panic it induced would be wicked and impossible to explain, especially to an officer of the law who probably knew English as well as Gary knew French which was zilch.

Vroom! Gary could hear the engine accelerating.

Cheery lights flashing.

"Arret!" came the order in French again from the cruiser PA on the roof but Gary kept running.

"Stop!" He heard in English which terrified Gary more, thinking whatever the policeman wants is more serious than he originally imagined, so he ran harder.

A garbage truck emptied a load and dropped the bin in the alley almost on top of Gary as he sprinted around the corner. The bin clipped his briefcase. Resumes sailed through the air. The dudgeon of doom opened and wasn't even 9 o' clock yet Gary realised and screamed. The police car screeched. The constable jumped out of the car, cuffs in hand, ready to make a bust when the hophead went lunatic spastic, rolling trying to protect himself from invisible mutants, screaming

"LEAVE ME ALONE!"

Gary wailed as the constable tried to grab the lunatic hophead now—

"I DIDN'T' DO ANYTHING!"

*****

The only positive about the psychiatric hospital was it was a great distance from where she lived so it was safe no one Felicity ever knew in her whole life growing up in Montreal would ever see she was here.

Her father Ray's presence was welcomed for safety and moral support. Daddy was built like a football player and was a no-nonsense straight arrow. If you rubbed him the wrong way or he thought you were a bum, he gave you a piece of his mind, no holding back.

Felicity loved her daddy but unless he was socializing with construction workers, felt he didn't have tact with people unlike himself. She did find it amusing how protective her daddy was when it came to dating boys.

When guys started paying serious attention to his super beautiful daughter in high school, he insisted she invite every young man home for dinner where he stared them down and grilled them to double check they had sincere intentions.

Her daddy liked hockey games on the weekends and home cooked meals her nanna specially prepared for him.

Ray still slicked his jet black hair back in an Elvis inspired pompadour. He also had French movie star Alain Delon blue eyes. Her nanna May told Felicity girls were crazy about him when he was a black leather jacket tough growing up in the '60s in North-end Montreal.

After her mom perished in a car accident, Daddy and Grandmother raised her. She felt sorry for her daddy stuck with her grandmother like he was married to her instead of ever finding a new wife for himself to love again.

Dr. Epps was an English guy about the same age as her daddy and looked more basketball player than psychiatrist.

Felicity wanted to cry when she looked at her daddy staring heartbroken, fighting to hold back tears as he listened to Dr. Epps calmly explain why she couldn't be released.

The last time she had seen him look so sad was years ago when she was a little girl and his wife, Felicity's mother, met her untimely fate and if it not for her Matriarch headstrong Grandmother, their loss would have ruined the family.

Felicity's grandmother May stared at the psychiatrist, arms crossed, nodding her head. When she heard what happened to her one and only sensitive, granddaughter, she was in such shock Ray had to rush her to the hospital where she was given oxygen.

Since then, May had regained her bearings and was not buying a lot of this English, psychobabble gobbledygook the imposing Doctor of Psychiatry was selling.

When May was young, she was a dead ringer for Katherine Hepburn and leveraged that to live a carousing life in the supper clubs and dance halls of Montreal, dating any man she encountered that struck her fancy during the wild ride of life in her youth. She had been married 4 times.

Ray was a love child from a brief but passionate affair she had with an Algerian painter, a dashing, handsome devil who looked like movie actor Omar Sheriff.

May lived by her own rules before the feminist zeitgeist empowered any woman in the modern world and thumbed her nose at sneering hypocrites who did the same or worse behind closed doors.

She once had a graceful body like her granddaughter but over the years put on considerable weight and now looked the part of Matron. Blessedly, her complexion remained

Katherine Hepburn pristine and very pretty for a woman of 86. And you could minus more years to her fiery disposition that never burnt out.

It had been 5 days since Felicity had been institutionalised. Tag dangling from her wrist. Sheet sluffing from her body. Other Patients wandered around. Some stared off into spaces beyond their lonely little worlds.

The medication numbed her and she was feeling increasing despair but didn't disclose this to the doctors for fear they would commit her for good. Ray rushed to console Felicity as she abruptly broke down.

"I want to go home with my grandmother and dad," Felicity demanded. The psychiatrist replied in the most compassionate tone he could:

"Felicity, you have to understand, you've experienced mental illness and are sick."

"I am not!" Felicity answered and cried.

"I'm sorry, you're not going to be able to leave."

"Why? Why not?" Felicity cried.

"You attempted to take your life," he calmly enunciated.

Tears came to May's eyes watching Felicity weep in Ray's arms.

"I realise the prospect of being in a facility can be unsettling…" Dr. Epps added.

"Then please let me go," Felicity begged.

"I promise following therapy you'll be better," he explained.

"Doctor, we've had difficult years and moved on,"
May added.

"I'd like to discuss that with Felicity," he answered.

Now Ray interjected.

"You're just going to open old wounds."

"We may have to for Felicity to recover," he said.

"You're wrong—all of you," Felicity yelled back.

The psychiatrist, May and Ray exchanged glances.

"Why do you say that, Felicity?" May jumped in.

"I'm almost 30 years old and have never even had a single boyfriend!" Felicity cried out. Again, the three of them exchanged looks.

"You're a beautiful, young woman. There will be many more opportunities," Dr. Epps replied.

"You don't get it! If you keep me here and say I'm crazy I'll never find a boyfriend if he finds out!"

Felicity sobbed. Ray held his weeping daughter, his construction worker macho face, tear-stained too.

May want to break down herself. But, there was no way she was going to let this ruin Felicity. No damn way. It was nothing short of tragic. Her beautiful, kind, loving, sensitive granddaughter in shambles.

She was determined to not let this unfortunate episode destroy Felicity, who she felt completely undeserving of this and much too soft for this often cold and cruel world. She would shield her granddaughter with a resolute optimism and verve that was the driving force that empowered her own character and being to survive for 86 years.

Chapter 3

The priest said his final words as they lowered the casket into the hole. Groundskeepers were already preparing to cover the casket and grave with dirt.

"He was the last friend, I had. Now, there's no one left," Harry uttered. The priest rested a consoling hand on Harry's shoulder. Paddy was 90, 4 years senior. Harry could justify losing him after such a long life, but the void it left would be considerable. Now. Everyone Harry ever knew—gone.

Harry was in a depressive daze as he rode the Metro towards home. He looked at a group of young people laughing. A young man consoling his wife that was with child. Two smitten lovers in the corner of the subway car, gazing into each other's eyes.

If only he could go back. He'd given everything he'd have just for one day to be young and in love like that. There had been a few women over the course of his life. All of them years and years apart. But the timing was never right. He had missed the boat with all of them. He was 86 years old and had nobody.

What happened to me? Where the hell did my life go, he despaired. As he left the Lionel Groulx Metro station, a panhandler asked for change. The guy must have been 20.

How could an able-bodied young man in his prime be begging like that?

For 50 years Harry worked. Delivering bonbon baked goods. Bonbon once had a monopoly on the Montreal market. Their brand name breads, cookies, and cakes in every dépanneur on the island. Twenty-one years since he retired now.

They had a pension plan. He had his little house paid off and was comfortable. His last friends always said he was lucky never having kids or ever being married. No pressure to struggle financially in order to feed and support a family.

But watching all the people he knew die over the last 10 years was hell and he realised how wrong they all were now that his aloneness was growing increasingly difficult to cope and manage.

He had hundreds and spent thousands and thousands of dollars on old DVD movies. When he watched, they helped transport him back to the old times when he was a younger and happier man.

He popped on a Rock Hudson and Doris Day romance.

The only time Harry had a smile on his face was when he saw Rock and Doris living and loving away. It wasn't working now though. Rock and Doris. The early '60s. An innocent age.

Montreal and the world was not the same place.

His favourite movie actor Rock Hudson being queer in the end. Dream girl Doris Day memories fleetingly fading as his youth. The world was all mucked up now. Young people always with their heads down on a phone walking and bumping into him while texting.

You couldn't get by in the world without a mobile phone now. He couldn't even walk to the bank to pay bills. Everything was done electronically.

The modern world didn't cater to his old ways and could give a damn if he couldn't keep up. He was a dinosaur in a world revolving around a phone or the internet.

What he resented most is it destroyed love.

The Rock Hudson and Doris style romance from his prime was gone. Young people sent naked pictures of each other over phones before even meeting. If you didn't qualify, they'd swipe to the next.

Society had changed, and he did not have any place in it.

He couldn't figure out how to keep up with the ways of gadgets. Now he was being timed out.

So Harry went to the cupboard to extract a bottle. He'd been resorting to this a few years since memories of his youth associated with the movie collection didn't give him the lift anymore. Drinking away the blues made him numb. An effective coping mechanism but it was going to kill him.

I'm going to die alone from a 'big drunk', he thought.

And the only reason they're going to know is the smell will be vile when his body rots.

*****

Gary spent the last week in a sedated state to recover from his breakdown. They didn't have any clocks, and he was trying to link on to a facility's elusive Wi-Fi.

He had the Montreal Urban Community transit app on his phone. His lifeline to the city was his bus pass. Without it, he would be trapped. Its access gave chances to improve life. Being Sunday service on routes was reduced, so Gary wandered around politely asking patients if they knew the time.

He met Glen again. Gary had been housed here twice since being in Montreal. First for a psychiatric assessment. Second for a retooling of his medication during an anxiety attack. It looked like Glen and his buddies never left.

"It's the Valentine's Day, birthday boy!" Glen yelled out.

"You remembered my birthday?" Gary responded.

"February 14th. St. Valentine. Patron Saint of Lovers,"

Glen announced while his group of buddies and sidekicks whispered in conference. Gary had nice memories of his Valentine's Day birthday.

"Mom made chocolate cupcakes with pink icing hearts on my Valentine's birthday, and I took them to elementary school and the whole class loved them," Gary said.

Glen consulted with his buddies while Gary waited. They were always talking about the good, the bad, and the ugly. Or God, the Devil and Buddha.

"You're predestined to be lucky in love, my friend,"

Glen smiled. *Hmm,* Gary thought. He liked a few girls in places, but love hadn't happened. Then the whole group of conspiracy theorists or Bible experts all smiled, and Glen pointed towards a woman at the other end of the room. She was seated, looking out the large window. Her golden hair was wrapped in a long pony tail, and her back was half turned so Gary could not see her face.

"Ask her, for the precise time." Glen told Gary.

The Bible experts were all grinning. Gary wondered why.

"C'mon, go for it," Glen said.

In the five days he had been here, he had never seen her.

Patients who were very sick or confused were locked and not permitted to mingle. Gary began to approach the woman sitting near the edge.

"The real sickos are quarantined," Gary remembered Glen Telling him.

"Excuse me, Miss. Do you have the time?" he said.

She turned to look, and *Oh My God,* Gary thought as he instantly froze, stunned. Tears were rolling down her cheeks and she looked like a model. A movie star?

Was the most beautiful girl he had ever seen in his life, causing his heart to miss a few beats. *How could a woman like her even be in a place like this,* he thought?

"You speak French," she said in a sweet Quebecois accent. Over the last few months, Gary learned some words and to say just one sentence in French.

"The only thing I know is *Voulez-vous Poulet Fries Au La Kentucky*." She laughed.

"How do you get to the Kentucky Fried Chicken," she said translating it into English.

"Yes," Gary said.

"That is the only thing I know how to say in French," he said.

He is cute, Felicity thought.

God, Gary thought to himself again, and his heart missed a few beats. *She is so, so beautiful. She must be an angel.*

Felicity wiped the tears from her face. *She's still looking at me too,* Gary thought.

"Why you crying?" Gary asked.

"This is my first time here."

Now she looked away and became sad again.

"And I'm scared I'm never going to get out."

"No, no, no. Don't be sad," Gary interjected.

He wanted to touch her on the shoulder at least but couldn't. Again, because she was way too perfect.

"I've visited these places all over. In many provinces and always get out."

"All over Canada?"

"Yes."

"You mean like insane asylum tourism," Felicity asked.

"Yes," he said.

Felicity laughed, "That's why I was trying to find out if you have the time. So I can find out when Bus 125 runs. On Sundays, most people don't work so the schedule's screwed up."

Who is this guy? What's he doing here? And boy, are his puppy dog eyes ever cute, she thought. *Wow,* again Gary thought.

Can't believe she keeps looking at me and smiling with those movie star teeth.

Dr. Epps, the chief psychiatrist in charge, entered.

"Excuse the intrusion? You two having a nice chat?"

"Yes, but I don't know her, sir," Gary added.

Felicity took Gary's hand and shook it.

"Felicity."

"Gary," he added.

She shook my hand. She's a normal person. She doesn't belong here. I must be way more crazy than her because I never would have the guts to shake a pretty girl's hand like that, he thought to himself.

"So, Gary. How are things?" Dr. Epps inquired.

"Fine."

"At terms with the experience that brought you here?"

"Yes."

"And?"

"I thought they were trying to come and get me."

"Now how do you feel?"

"I know it's not true."

"I suppose you're clear. Clean bill of health. Ready to go?" Dr. Epps asked.

"For sure," Gary said. He looked at Felicity.

"Even though you didn't have the time, nice meeting you."

"Yes, nice knowing you've toured lots of loony bins and were always able to escape," Felicity replied.

An old woman patient shuffled by. SHU-SHU-SHU sound from her slippers. She stopped to look at Gary.

"You better dress up good if you're going outside to wait for the bus, otherwise you'll get the sniffles."

An orderly entered. Felicity and Gary shared felt the same sad sensation. They ever going to be able to see each other again?

"Time to roll, bro," the Black orderly chided.

Gary glanced back as the orderly accompanied him off the floor. He was looking at Felicity, and she was looking at him.

She didn't want him to leave.

He didn't want to go.

He wished he was sick so he could stay.

All she knew is she wanted him to stay.

Tears rolled down Felicity's cheeks again.

That guy may be my mister perfect, and now he's gone?

Chapter 4

When he didn't drink the blues away and the memories associated from the Rock Hudson and Doris Day DVD movies from the good old days didn't work, Harry headed for Mount Royal to walk around the park and listen to the birds sing.

October was his favourite time to visit. Humid summer heat gone. Relax on the bench. Watch life go by breathing crisp clean fall air. Beaver Lake lovers in short sleeves riding in rented mini boats, snuggling up. Families sashaying by.

Kids laughing frolicking in fallen leaves. Joggers sprinting through trails. Lovers hand-in-entranced. Harry snapped a few shots of red and gold hued fallen foliage leaves with his camera.

It began with this little bird. In fact, he was pretty damn sure he was seeing the same damn, little sparrow, hanging around chirping all the time. And, this little bird seemed to be looking right at him. Harry took a few snap shots of it.

Either he was losing his mind or something, but he was pretty sure this was the same bird he'd seen visiting Mont Royal Park during the late summer and in September. He snapped another photo of it. Later on, he'd compare the plumage marks on the bird in close up pictures and determine if it was the same one.

If it was following him around it was an omen. Good one he hoped. Harry laughed. Nonsense. No damn friends. No relatives. Nobody left to know him. This chirping little bird had eyes on him and was the only creature that acknowledged his existence. I gotta be going nuts. *If this was the onset of senility I'm toast,* he thought.

Harry's parents had lived to their late 80s, and their minds were sharp through and through so he had been blessed with health, longevity, and good genes. And now this little bird, chirping, his only source of comfort to help ride out last lonely days in the sunset of his life without love.

Then he spotted something peculiar. A young man was feeding squirrels. Harry had seen children tossing bits of foods to animals, but this was a lone young man in his 20s. His face lit up with joy up as he fed them and it looked like he was gently speaking to the squirrels cavorting around him. Now the young guy was approaching.

He looked spaced out. He was gazing around. Looking at children. Up at the sky. Into the trees as if he was having a conversation with them. And he was in awe. Bizarre. All these young people now with their phones and computers like they were connected to their bellybuttons. This young guy had no device. *He was plugged into nature,* Harry thought.

Benches were taken, but there was a vacant spot beside an old man sitting by himself. Gary didn't want to sit down on the grass because it was damp, so he walked up.

"Bonjour, hello. May I sit?" Gary said.

"You English?" Harry shot back.

"How'd you know?"

"No Quebecois twang."

"Yup, I don't know French."

Holy crap, a lone English guy like himself roaming around loose in 'Mon-ree-all', Harry thought.

"Sit down."

"Thanks," Gary replied and sat.

Harry evaluated him again. Clean clothes. Clean-cut. Sounds like he's not on dope. What's this guy's story?

"I see you like the squirrels."

"Yes, feed them left over bread."

A little sparrow flew over and danced by Harry's feet. The sparrow stopped. Looked up at Harry and uttered tweet-tweet. Gary laughed. Harry took a few snap shots of it.

"Got ya," Harry said.

"You know that bird or something," Gary asked.

"Know when I compare the feathers in photos taken over the past few weeks." The sparrow buzzed off. Circled and flew back again.

"That bird knows you," Gary said.

"We must be acquainted from another life."

Gary didn't smell liquor on his breath and thought maybe this old guy is drunk?

"That possible," Gary asked.

"In reincarnation belief system," Harry answered.

Harry had been hooked on eschatology a few years back, but it passed before he himself did. *The old guy marches to the tune of a different drummer all right,* Gary thought.

"The name is Harry."

"Hi, I'm Gary."

Harry explained his hobby was photography. That he took close-up and long shots of nature. Animals. City landmarks. Heritage architecture, then later developed them in a dark room he had at home.

"Used to work for that company who made that bread your squirrels are munching on. Do that often, it can be a pretty expensive hobby," Harry added.

Gary explained he did it with left over bread at the end of the month. The day before a carefully planned grocery shopping because he was on a limited budget.

"What are your vices? You chase peroxide blondes?" Harry joked.

"Ahh, no," Gary answered.

"So, you're all alone, just like me?"

"Yea."

"Why's that? A handsome, young guy like you?"

"All my friends are dead."

"Dead—how?" Harry barked.

"Killed in Afghanistan."

"You were in the army?"

"Yes," Gary added.

"All your buddies gone?"

"Everyone in my squad."

Harry looked at Gary. He was serious.

"Join the club, partner. All my friends are dead too."

"From what?"

"Ammonia. Aneurysms. Ailments and afflictions of the aorta — pretty much natural causes."

"You well, Mister?"

"Me? I'm too bull-headed to die."

"Mind me asking, how old are you?" Gary inquired.

"Guess?" Harry answered.

Gary studied him. He looked pretty healthy for an old guy. Was full of pep and spark. Lots of porcupine white hair sticking up. Only real deep wrinkles he had were deep frown lines between his eyebrows. Gary thought he got those because he'd probably been sad in life.

"I don't know, seventy? Seventy-one?" Gary replied.

"86."

"86! Wow! What's your secret?"

"Hard work and cleaning living."

Maybe his wife died? Or if he never had a wife, was scary, Gary thought.

"That's how you stayed in good shape?"

"Plus I never took dope. Nor smoked a single cigarette my whole life."

Gary smiled.

"Neither have I," Gary said.

"Birds of a feather," Harry added.

Gary stuck out his hand. "Friends?"

"You betcha." Harry shook Gary's hand.

"Especially since my days are numbered," Harry added.

"Don't say that," Gary said to keep things upbeat.

"You only get so many points in your account," Harry concluded.

It was the first time Harry had a conversation with a fellow human being in months, and he invited Gary to come over to his place. Gary was visiting Mont Royal because it was the end of the month and the Sweetest Day but he could have dessert tomorrow and not having any job to report to nor knowing anyone else, there was no reason for him to say no.

They took a bus from the Mount Royal Parking Lot to Berri-UQUAM. Then the green to line Lionel Groulx station. Harry and Gary rode the 211 bus to the west island of Montreal.

Harry lived in the Montreal district of Dorval. During the 2-minute stroll from the bus stop to Harry's bungalow, they passed a shopping plaza that included a hair salon, bank, liquor store, licensed lounge, and megabox supermarket. Harry said the easy proximity to these amenities kept him fed and watered during the cold winter months when he didn't venture downtown much.

Gary observed the construction design of housing in the Dorval area contrasted compared to apartment, walk-up front stairs style housing that predominated in central Montreal and marvelled at all airplanes taking off and landing from nearby Pierre Elliot Trudeau airport, as they ambled to where Harry lived.

"King-sized coffee in a king sized cup for my new friend," Harry said as he handed the mug of brew to Gary admiring framed black and white photos of heritage architecture in Harry's bungalow living room.

"Montreal's heyday in the late fifties," Harry added.

"Lots of fancy neon lights," Gary commented sipping on coffee.

"In the '50s, Montreal was lit up like Vegas."

Gary continued to turn pages of the photo album.

"Those buildings are torn down now. That world is no more."

"Have any people pictures?"

"Yea."

"Can I see them?"

"Why? You wouldn't know anyone?"

"Maybe you can find some friends still alive?"

Harry returned with an arm full of albums. As Gary turned the pages and pointed to individuals, Harry responded.

"Dead."

"Him?"

"Dead."

"This guy?"

"Goner too."

"This guy in the bathing suit?"

"Move to Florida then croaked." Harry was growing upset.

"Don't be so discouraged."

"I told you everyone's dead!"

"Why so snappish?"

"Because it's depressing as hell!"

"I was just trying to give you hope."

"Hope! The devil is coming to get me!"

"Unless St. Peter rescues you first," Gary added.

Harry laughed. He really made a new friend. There might be someone to bury him now when he was gone.

"You ever married?" Gary asked.

"No."

"Why not?"

Harry shook his head.

"Could you explain?"

"Why," he said growing increasingly exasperated now.

"Didn't see any pictures of girls?"

"Just make me more miserable if I do."

"You gay?"

"I don't believe this!"

Harry picked up another photo album and opened it. Various photos of men and women.

"Satisfied?"

"They're couples. Anyone ever your girl?"

"Doesn't matter," Harry kept turning the pages.

"Not even one?"

Harry tossed the photo album aside. Gary could see he looked really blue.

"What about a girl you have no picture of?"

Harry stopped frowning and thought. Now he smiled.

"What?" Gary asked.

Harry returned 5 minutes later with a cardboard box full of unorganised photos and was sifting through it when he pulled one out. He wiped the dust off it. Looked at the picture and smiled for the 2nd time today. It was a black and white school photo of children.

"Someone from way back you remember?"

"French gal I dream about from time-to-time."

"What happened?"

"I was in love with her, but she got away."

Gary glanced at the picture Harry was holding. It was a kindergarten class photo. Children attentively looking forward except a little boy in suspenders and a giggling little girl in a dress smiling at each other instead of staring straight like the class. Harry pointed to the little boy and girl.

"Me and her."

It was so blatant Gary was stunned.

"How long ago this picture taken?" Harry laughed.

"About 80 years ago."

"Maybe you can find her. Maybe she's not dead."

"Had my chance but blew it."

"Try again!"

"Went round two with her years later and lost again."

"What do you mean?"

"She ended up marrying someone else."

"How long ago?"

"40–45 years ago."

"Maybe her husband's gone!"

"You nuts?"

"Maybe you can love her again!"

Harry smiled. Imagine that, then dismissed the thought.

"Why don't you look up one of your old flames?"

"Can't."

"Why not? You gay?"

"No, never had a girlfriend."

"Better find a lady friend before it's too late."

"Huh," Gary asked, bemused.

"Or you'll end up like me!"

Harry tossed the school photo on the coffee table.

Gary picked it back up.

"Look at you both! It was meant to be!"

"We were like 6 or 8 years old," Harry said.

"Pure puppy love."

Harry thought way back. Gary's words were true.

"It's going to hurt like hell when I learn she's dead."

"You can find that information out?"

After digging through boxes 10 minutes later Harry dropped a telephone book on the table. Front page identified it circa 1980.

Harry blew the dust off it. Opened to flip pages. Stopped and began running his finger down a list of French surnames.

"Got it."

"You sure? That was fast?"

"I know the bugger who married her and approximate area they lived."

Gary handed over the phone. Harry proceeded to punch the numbers.

"It's ringing."

"Good luck," Gary responded.

May was drying dishes from the late lunch she prepared for her son Ray on his way out to an afternoon shift on a condominium under construction when the phone rang. Ray glanced at the caller ID and didn't recognise the number but picked it up because it could be medically related to Felicity being released from the hospital tomorrow.

"Oui?" Ray said in French.

On the other end of the line, Harry was ready:

"My name is Harry. I'm trying to locate May."

Silence. Harry waited for a reply.

"What? Who are you?" Ray requested in French.

"Pard me, my French is shaky. Could you please parlez-vouz in English," Harry kindly petitioned.

"What do you want, sir?" Ray uttered in an unfriendly English tone.

"I'm trying to contact May. I know her from way back."

Again, Harry waited. Ray turned to look at his mother drying dishes and cupped the phone receiver to respond.

"How do you know her?" he inquired, again in an unfriendly English tone.

"To be blunt, we used to be a couple back in the day."

"You're telling me my mom used to be your girlfriend?"

Ray looked at May out of earshot turning on the sink to rinse a pot.

"Yes," Harry replied dead serious.

"Which one? Number 10? 20," Ray snapped back ready to hang up. Gary sensed the person on the other line said something that hurt.

"Please," Harry said.

Ray glanced at his mother drying dishes, now looking over. May sensed something of significance. By the expression on her son's face confirmed something was up?

"We went on a few dates. Then Big John stepped in the picture and married her before I could," Harry added.

"John was my stepdad. Don't you disgrace his memory because he's dead."

On the other end of the line, joy surged through Harry's being and he smiled for a 3rd time today.

"Dead."

"Big John gone too?"

"Harry? I never heard of no English guy named 'Harry'?"

"I'm hanging up," Ray said.

May snatched the receiver from Ray just in time.

"Who is this," she demanded in English.

The moment Ray heard her sultry voice he knew it was her and he smiled for the 4th time today. That was a record. He had not smiled 4 times in one day for years. At least not since he watched a hard-to-get Rock Hudson and Doris Day romantic comedy that released from the Hollywood vault onto DVD.

"May, it's Harry."

"Harry? I only ever knew one 'Harry' and he used to be in my kindergarten class years ago."

"Yes, that's it. The one and only me,"

An inner spark lit in May.

One she hadn't felt since she was a little girl.

If she could pinpoint and articulate this sweetness, it simply would be pure puppy love.

"Hello? Hello?" Harry barked now.

Desperate he'd been cut off or hung up on.

"May, it's really me, from back in the day."

She was still stunned but now smiling.

"May! It's me—Harry! Hello? May?"

"Impossible," May answered in a daze.

"Swear it! I'm telling you—it's me, Harry!"

Ray was watching the reaction on his mom's face. Although in her mid-eighties, she was still an assertive powerhouse, and had been rattled by whoever was on the other line on the phone, clearly spooking him.

"But the last time I saw you…" May said.

"Ogilvy's department store on St. Catharines Street."

"Yes, I remember," May said in French.

The look on his mom's face. He'd never seen it before.

Ray was really worried.

"I'm sorry. Was never much for speaking French."

"Yes, I remember," she added.

Which was unfortunate because he was quite sentimental, she recollected.

"Yea, you once called me a romantic, English fool,"

May smiled wistfully.

"Then, when you told me you were marrying Big John, I had no choice but to walk away."

"John has since passed, 10 years now."

With the conversation going Gary was smirking and silently cheering Harry on.

"Didn't dream I'd see you again. We should meet up?"

That would be nice, she thought.

"Sure, bring your wife along to visit."

When Harry heard that, he froze. His expression was so deep it gave Gary jitters.

"What? What is it? She hang up?" Gary asked.

Harry had to take a breather before he spoke.

"May, I have something to tell you. I don't have a wife."

She was stunned silent.

"Sorry to hear. When did she pass?"

Again, Harry had to stop to compose himself.

"May, I'm still single. I never married."

A feeling. Kindergarten 80 years ago. Innocence. Wonderful. Sweet, sweet love.

Then she recalled the heartbroken look on Harry's face telling him she was marrying John and became tearful.

"What is it? What did he say?" Ray urged her in French.

Ignoring Ray, May replied to Harry on the phone.

"When you have a pen I will give the address. You're welcome to come for Thanksgiving dinner alone or with a guest."

What was she thinking? Ray had never seen his tough cookie of a mom in a daze like this. What began as a farce was turning damn scary. Harry placed the receiver down and stared at stunned.

"Lord sweet thundering Jesus..."

"What?" Gary asked.

"She invited me to dinner!"

"Woo-woo," Gary cheered.

"I'm going to need all the help I can get."

"Why?" Gary asked confused.

"In case I have to exit lickety-split."

"I don't get it."

He had to focus on good and be optimistic now.

"You bring me good luck. Your idea was good, kid. You're coming with me, right?"

Gary replied with a smile.

Ray was spooked. His mom was wild when she was young and had many flings, but this English speaking Harry guy was in a separate category. Had some strange effect on her.

"You okay?"

"Yes."

"You sure? I can stay home. The job's done."

"No, you go ahead to work."

Ray kissed his mom bye on the cheek and scampered off.

May sat in the kitchen reminiscing. She had lost contact with him twice. As a little girl when her family moved to another part on the island of Montreal she cried for him. Years later she bumped into him delivering racks of bread in a grocery store where he promptly asked her out.

Even as a single Mom dragging her young boy Ray around, was never short of suitors throwing themselves at her. To discourage Harry she told him the truth. She'd been married 3 times. Was engaged to John. Harry didn't care. Declared his love and still wanted her. In the end, she chose to betroth, big debonair John and still recollected the heartbroken expression on Harry's face. How crushed he was.

Not the typical type of man she dated. Stout. Shorter than her, but nice looking and gushing with feeling. An oddball who wore his heart on his sleeve. He was difficult to understand and she was caught off guard by his affection at the time. Thanksgiving was next week. She couldn't wait to see how he turned out after all these years. No way she was going to be unnerved if Harry showed the same tenderness towards her now.

Chapter 5

Felicity responded favourably to a change in medication and was released to the custody of her grandmother and father.

Dr. Epps cautioned them she could be vulnerable to relapse if was exposed to similar stress. When he recommended Felicity remain home May protested.

Felicity would recover best if she went back to work like nothing ever happened. 2 days following her release, Ray parked a few blocks from the Outremont Ballet Academy and turned to look at his daughter smiling in the back seat.

"Sure about this now," he asked in French.

"Everything except how I'm going to explain my absence,"

Felicity replied.

"Tell Hanna the truth," he added in English.

Hanna was a Russian who founded the internationally renowned Outremont Ballet Academy. She was a classically trained ballerina and gymnast who came to Montreal to compete in the 1976 Olympics. The Russians had a fit when she refused to return to Moscow suspecting cold war high treason when the reality was she met the man of her dreams in Montreal and settled for love.

"No messages. No phone calls. Your students were restless and out of control. I was unable to get in touch with you? Thank goodness Nancy covered the whole time."

It was as difficult leaving the psychiatric hospital as entering. Now, to explain her absence to people whose opinions she placed a high value on. How was she ever going to account for the desperate action she took to take her life?

"May I be honest and lay my cards on the table."

"Yes, we absolutely need an explanation for the absence?"

"I was sick…"

Hanna just stared at her.

"It was a slight emotional breakdown."

Hanna comprehended the gist immediately. Felicity was an exceedingly sensitive and physically responsive little girl who blossomed into a world-class super beauty and dancer and that talent was susceptible to shattering because her essence was internally fragile.

"You need to realise something: the children under our tutelage have parents who are well-to-do, important people."

"I'm sorry," Felicity added.

"You under a doctor's care?"

"I'm seeing a psychiatrist."

"Some parents may not be so understanding."

"I promise it won't happen again."

Felicity's soft eyes and expression conveyed sorrow more powerfully than she ever could verbalise it. To Hanna, Felicity was the daughter she never had.

"Either way, welcome back,"

Hanna added with a smile. Felicity responded hugging her mentor tight.

With the exception of that uncomfortable moment, Felicity's first day back went superb. Ballerinas cheered when her demonstration left them awed and inspired. But some parents questioned her disappearance? She almost broke down when a father pressed for details concerning her protracted absence till Nancy intervened with verbal dance steps, or 'bullshit' she later laughed about in order to defuse him.

During Felicity's vanishing, rumours circulated she was in jail. Had been using credit cards fraudulently to expand her wardrobe. That she was pregnant. Later aborted the baby.

Had contracted a virulent sexually transmitted disease.

Her best friend Nancy endured it all, being sworn to secrecy and knowing the truth, unable to defend Felicity from the abominable lies.

"I am so ashamed. No one will ever treat or respect me the same after what happened," Felicity said.

"Don't give a hoot if that ballerina's bigwig Dad is a utility company executive. I know you were in pain. It was none of his business cross-examining you about your absence."

"Thanks for covering my back when I was gone."

"I should have been there for you that night. You were the only one who supported me when the rest of them refused to believe my ex was screwing around," Nancy answered.

Felicity and Nancy hugged like true sisters. After work, they went for drinks on Crescent Street. They had wine, cheese, and chatted to catch up.

Everyone at the Outremont Ballet Academy was excited when it was announced esteemed New York choreographer Juan Sanchez was casting for this season's rendition of the Nutcracker to be held at Montreal's very own Place Des Arts.

Rumours were circulating and some resented it, but every dancer knew Felicity had the best chance to get the leading female role. Then hello Broadway and the road to International dance stardom.

*****

Nancy pulled up to Felicity's grandmother's house and stopped the car, Felicity hugged her again.

"Thanks so much for your support when I slipped," tear-stained Felicity said. Nancy always built her and fellow dancers up. Never uttered unkind things unless they drew first blood.

*****

Felicity lay in bed entertaining aspirations nourished since she was 6 years old.

Years preparing. Conditioning. Dieting. Stretching. Relentless repetition rehearsing. She was 29 years old. In her physical prime.

World-renowned Broadway Choreographer Juan Sanchez coming to Montreal.
'The Nutcracker' her big break.
She was ready to shine.
All the pieces were falling into place.
Except, she was still alone.
There was no Mr. Perfect.

Chapter 6

The Garelli Brothers were twins of Middle Eastern origin who began as venture capitalists into acquisition of real estate that evolved into residential and office tower development in Eastern American seaboard cities of Boston and New York.

Two years after they expanded into Montreal transforming the city skyline. Tax incentives. Lower Canadian dollar. Cheap land. Demand for high rise residential urban living, a boon to them.

Dick was 35, square-jawed, slicked-back brown hair, tailor-trimmed suits, cuff links, perpetually tanned, and exuded the confidence of a champion. He was also considered one of the most sought after bachelors in Montreal's French-Canadian social circle networks.

Though graduating at the top of his Law class at McGill University, Dick considered the term 'Lawyer' a dirty word. What differentiated his consultancy from other sharks was he never failed, was a man of action who accomplished results. To clients, he was a facilitator.

He expedited things. Cut crap, red tape, bullshit, formalities. Anything obstructing the smooth flow of money. Not a problem. Leave it to me. Let me worry about the headache, were personal mantras he subscribed to.

Many of his alma mater where leaders in Montreal's business community and relationships with them ensured access and favours.

When stonewalled, Dick delegated the matter to the best and brightest and later presented simple answers to clients who compensated him damn, good money.

He had made a cool mill on services rendered off the Garelli Brothers since they entered the Montreal market and continued demand for residential high rise condo in the city core and townhouses in the environs ensured dough kept flowing.

It was as balmy outside as it was in Florida, so Dick drove up to the location in his convertible candy apple Vette with the roof and windows down while Ray was taking a 15-minute breather, sipping coffee.

"I understand you're the man?"

"Right, I'm in charge here," Ray replied in French.

Dick stepped out.

"I'd like to shake your hand…"

Ray had never seen this suit in his life.

"Who are you?"

"New boss. You cost me serious dough," Dick said grinning.

"Sounds like a reason to shit-can me," Ray replied.

"You completed the Atwater Condo two weeks ahead of schedule."

Ray smiled. They shook hands.

"Nice tan."

"Just got back from Tampa Bay," Dick smiled.

"Raymond."

"Pleasure to make your acquaintance," Dick responded.

Clean cut. Fancily dressed. Soft hand shake but firm grip. Who is this beach bum? Ray thought.

"Represent Garelli Brothers Properties. We recently acquired your construction outfit," Dick said in English.

He's Anglophone, and his French is perfect, Ray thought.

"And I'd like you to personally oversee future projects for us," he continued in French.

"Why's that?" Ray responded in English.

"Overlooked unsigned permits from city hall. If you didn't spot that it would have prevented residents from moving into their luxury properties earlier than promised," Dick said in English.

Bosses from the old days never acknowledged a job well done, odd coming from this young guy likely spoiled by too much good life in the sun, Ray thought.

"Don't go anywhere without my guys."
"The offer is just open to you?"
"My guys backed me up for years. If they're out, no deal."
"Fine, but one condition: they have to pass a performance test," Dick conditionally added.
"Why the high standards?"
"New Millennium. Competition. Downsizing. Cutbacks. Retrenchment. Dog-eat-dog. Survival of the fittest."
"I have to jump this wall too?" Ray asked.
"You've demonstrated strengths and are exempt."
"How much raise in pay we talking here?" Ray asked.
"70,000 dollars salary per annum," Dick replied.
"I'll do it for 70,000 a year pay after tax," Ray answered.
"Done."
They had drinks in La Salle at a bar a few blocks away.
Dick outlined compensation and expanded on the Garelli Brothers mandate to build all over the Island of Montreal.

His ideas sound smart, but he's not a worker. Clean hands. No dirty finger nails. Talks about building but has probably never picked up a hammer in his life, Ray thought.

Dick's mobile buzzed,
"Excuse me."
Ray sipped beer while Dick spoke English to an individual on the other end of the line
"Think I'm going to let you put me in the position where I can be screwed and skinned alive… fine, it's over for good then."
Dick clicked off and shook his head.
"There's no honest women left in Montreal."
Ray quaffed his beer and placed the empty mug down.
"B.S.," Ray uttered.
"You know decent woman not out for a meal ticket."
"Yes."
"Who?"
"My daughter. She's in a league of her own. Not only a true beauty but an original innocent as well."
Dick downed the rest of his beer.
"Maybe we should get acquainted?"

"How do I know you're worthy?" Ray asked.

"How do I know you're not exaggerating?" Dick responded. Ray tossed pretzels in his mouth.

Thought about it as he munched.

"We're having Thanksgiving dinner. You're welcome to drop by. Meet Felicity."

Ray produced a pen. Scribbled a note.

"This is the address."

Dick accepted the note. Glanced at it.

"Greenfield Park, huh?"

"Forty-four years at the same address."

As Ray drove home, the more he thought about the idea, the more he liked it. If Felicity is attracted to this guy, he could really take her places. *Definitely, he definitely could be the jackpot for Felicity if she liked him,* Ray thought.

*****

Gary contemplated shifting seasons for the first time.

In Vancouver when days grew shorter and air damper, temperature change was subtle. As autumn advanced in Montreal, pleasant, sunny days of early October alternated with overcast clouds propelled by breezes with shivering chills.

Most evergreens were bereft leaves so the wind did not shake them in B.C. Separated leaves from deciduous trees danced circles in the streets of Montreal.

One mild, sunny afternoon Gary left his place, and the sky turned black an hour later. The wind howled and whistled so intensely it felt like it was cutting through him.

So bad he entertained ideas of returning West. He passed a charity thrift store by pure happenstance and purchased a puffy coat, pseudo wool mittens, and a jet black toque for 15 welfare dollars.

As residents cursed inclement conditions, Gary marvelled at differences in temperature he was experiencing during the change of seasons as a new resident. Balmy days alternated with ones previewing winter. Instead of dread, Gary relished learning you simply dress up when the wind whipped to not freeze your sissy, Vancouver butt off.

*****

Thank God, Thanksgiving arrived, Harry thought.

He and Gary rode in a cab across the St. Lawrence River to the suburb of Greenfield Park. *Why didn't I search? All this time at the same address? What a loss to not contact her years ago,* Harry thought and rang the bell.

"How do I look?"

"Like you're going to wedding a or a funeral. Good luck."

"Been to very few weddings and way too many funerals."

Harry literally had suited up for this. Hadn't worn the nifty black and white outfit and bow tie for years. The door opened.

May saw Harry and screamed—shocked.

"Hi."

"Harry—you look."

Harry smiled. *He has nice teeth,* she thought.

"How long has it been?" she asked.

"49 years."

"Hurry, come in."

Harry wiped his shoes.

"49 years?"

She looked him over and was stunned.

"49 years since I last saw you in Ogilvy's department store where we went for a coffee, and you broke the news you were marrying Big John."

A sad sentiment hit May.

Did she overlook him? Make a mistake?

The oddball she remembered sure aged well.

"Here you are again: just as lovely as ever," he said.

How can this be? Harry? Here? Now?

Dapper. Trim. Healthy.

Not the inept and insecure much younger man she remembered. She was not prepared for this.

"Get serious, I've put on tons of weight," she added.

She took Harry's coat. The way he smiled.
Obviously just as taken with her as he'd been years ago
"So you put on weight?
Again she faced him, smiling.
But—your face—it's just as beautiful like years ago!"
"No way? No way," she replied.
"Yes way," Harry answered beaming back.
She was flabbergasted.
Harry turned into one handsome old man.
86, she told herself.
Could love return so late?
Just like Harry fell out of the sky.

Gary witnessing them staring at each other and thought, *Very, very nice.* There was a purity about the idea of them.

The old lady liking him so much too.

Ray enters. Sees Harry and the way his mom was smiling? *What the hell is going on here,* he thinks.

A bridge built between her and some silver fox spiffed in a suit, bow tie, and flower attached to his lapel.

"No," Ray says reflexively, without even thinking.

The multitudes of gentleman callers his mom had over the years and he doesn't recognise this one? What is happening between her and his old-timer is real and very serious.

Harry snapped out of the love spell and glanced at Ray.

"This must be who I spoke to on the phone. Your son?"

Ray just nods, eyeing Harry suspiciously.

And then Felicity emerges.

Gary sees her, and just like the first time, his heart misses a few beats.

Felicity gasps. *My God. My maybe Mister Perfect,* she thinks astounded. What's he doing here?

Ray has now taken all of this in and is terrified.

Is unable to voice it but knows it is love his mother and daughter are feeling. His mother one thing, she had a life, but my one and only beautiful, innocent daughter.

If Ray had a pit bull, he'd order it to attack and chew them both up on the spot.

"My granddaughter, Felicity," May announced.

"Hi," Felicity said and extended her hand.

Instead of shaking her hand, Harry kissed it.

"What a beauty. Good looks run in the family. If May wasn't around and I was 50 years younger, I'd go for you myself."

Ray cringed. It was excruciating. He felt like screaming.

He glanced at Gary laying low in the alcove now.

"Who the hell is he?" Ray barked in English.

"My friend," Harry announced.

Felicity and Gary were all eyes, smiling away.

"How do you get to the Kentucky Fried Chicken?" Gary said in broken Quebecois to Felicity.

Felicity laughed.

Again, Ray thinks, *Marde. Who are these English freaks?*

"You know this guy?" Ray asked Felicity in French.

"From the hospital," she tells her dad.

The last thing Ray wants to hear. Worse than he imagined.

"Hospital? What were you guys in for?" Harry interjected.

"Don't answer," Ray addressed in French to protect Felicity.

"It's no secret. I had to be treated for an emotional breakdown," Felicity replied in English.

Few minutes later they were munching on finger food.

Carrots. Celery. Broccoli. Dipping chunks in mayo and garlic dip. Harry was open to potato chips but there was only ketchup flavour and he liked salt and vinegar, so he paged through the photo album he brought along.

All eyes were on the kindergarten picture.

May and Harry the only children in the group smiling at each other instead of staring straight at the camera like all the other pupils. Their puppy love irrefutably captured on film for history.

"Miss Picado's kindergarten class picture. May and I smirking away."

Ray scrutinized the portrait, munching on a garlic dipped carrot stick.

"I don't believe it."

Harry grimaced, recoiled from Ray's garlic breath.

"I didn't believe it either, Daddy. But look at the image. It's true," Felicity added.

"Yea, I tell you. May and I were really in love with each other way back then," Harry added.

May could not take her eyes off him; he looked so good.

"So many moons ago," May replied smiling.

Harry ignited feelings not felt for in her for decades.

Ray glared, discerning and loathing his mother's response.

May stared right at him. Forty-nine years. Damn it, she thought.

"Yea, great life. Great, great life," Harry said.

Years of emptiness. Why didn't he do something more?

Big John or not. He never should have stopped believing in the love he felt for her.

"You know what?" Felicity said.

"What?" Ray fired back.

"Maybe it's not over for them?"

A dead weight of loneliness left Harry that moment. Felicity's sweet voice uttering those words.

You angel, Harry thought looking at May's gorgeous granddaughter. May smiling. Always at ease when it came to interpersonal relations compared to his clumsy self.

So, Harry went for it.

Placed his hand on hers.

Shocked himself by the brazenness of it.

Why didn't he dare take action like this when he was a young and in his prime? May looked at Harry's hand resting on hers.

"Is that the way you feel?" May asked.

"Yes, that's the way I feel," Harry replied back.

"Memories," May said.

"Memories. And now… time left…" Harry added.

May looked deep into Harry's sad eyes and smiled again.

It was so unbelievable. The way he looked. Self-doubt and pain dissipated transformed to joy. Ray seethed witnessing it.

Whatever was happening between his mom and this old-timer was undeniable. He was going to butt-heads with this old coot who clearly would be a threat to his balanced and routine life.

"You know what I say?" Gary added.

"No, what do you say?" Ray uttered challenging him.

"The best things in life are free. Or under a dollar ninety-nine."

Felicity giggled. Gary liked the way she laughed and tossed a ketchup potato chip in his mouth.

This can't be happening. What a horror show. Love erupting from nowhere all around, Ray thought.

"Check the damn turkey before it's ruined," Ray snarled.

"Excuse me," May softly said to Harry who did not want to let go of her hand.

Ray followed May to the kitchen.

"You need to seriously calm down," she warned him.

"It's sickening. He's seducing you in our house in front of the whole family!"

May slapped Ray. He glared. Shocked. Stunned at her.

"Wipe that look off your face," May ordered.

"It's disgusting. You're my mother," Ray pleaded now.

"You know what it was like? Those years dragging me around? Men chasing you every-where?"

"You are not my husband," May fired back.

"You're 86—I thought it was over."

She wanted to smack him again.

"Him in that bow tie and flower. He's a snake!"

May wanted to cry. Her son had no idea who Harry was?

Her life filled with all those men and marriages. Harry alone all that time. The doorbell rang.

At last, Ray thought. His new boss, Dick. He stormed out to get the door and let his new boss in.

Chapter 7

After introductions with Dick, they ate. May glowered as Ray directed guests playing a game of musical chairs. He couldn't do much about Mom, but the last thing he wanted was his daughter falling for some mental case she met in a nut house.

Like a pre-emptive chess move, he made it awkward for Gary to encounter his daughter giving a clear path for Dick and Felicity to face each other instead. Here was Felicity's chance to meet a successful, responsible, intelligent gentleman she could start a life with.

And like so many other men, Dick could not take his eyes off the ravishing, beautiful daughter he was half responsible for creating. Ray felt perfectly justified giving Felicity to him.

If they were mismatched in the long-term, it would still be a win-win situation because Felicity would be set for life with this high roller if it didn't work out.

May watched Harry grow increasingly fidgety and uncomfortable. Playing with his food on the plate, exchanging self-conscious glances instead of smiles with her now.

How could he not have anticipated something that had occurred repeatedly over the years whenever he was invited out and there was no buffet style choice to eat?

"Why are you separating the beans, carrots, and corn on one side of the plate?" May asked.

"Not as hungry as I thought," he answered.

"You've hardly eaten a thing."

"Too many appetizers I guess."

"You only had a few chips."

"I had turkey."

"Have more turkey then."

"I'll pass."

"Why not?"

"Some spices aren't reacting well in my gut."

What's wrong? May thought. *Why was he suddenly so uptight? Thanksgiving was joyful, not some ordeal.*

"So is that your secret?" Dick asked.

"What?" Harry asked.

"You watch what you eat?"

"What do you mean?"

"How you stay in such good shape for a guy your age. You're particular about food?"

"Not at all. Just worked hard my whole life. Never sat around. Always active in motion. Loading. Lifting. Hauling. Shelving. Plus, I never abused myself. Never drank much till after I retired. And I never smoked."

"What about women?" Dick asked

"Guess never being married helped keep me stay young too."

Dick knew he was about to say something inappropriate, but Ray was tacitly goading him on with a smirk.

"The celibacy voluntary or involuntary?"

Ray burst out laughing. No one else found it amusing.

First May was undecided. He obviously was good-looking and came across well-mannered but as dashing and handsome as he was, May disapproved of Dick after that remark about Harry even though he would have been a great catch for Felicity.

Gary leaned to look at Felicity two seats beside him.

Ray shifted in his seat—blocking Gary's view yet again.

"What?" Ray gloating, asked Gary.

"You have ants in your pants," Gary replied.

Felicity laughed.

It was obvious her daddy kept repositioning his body when Gary tried to see her. She found the charade and her daddy's high standards when it came to guys he felt worthy of her always amusing.

"Can I offer you some mashed potatoes?" May asked Harry. Harry looked at them.

He liked potatoes but was sure he detected lumps in them.

"What kind of mashed potatoes we talking here?" Harry asked.

"Partial to mashed potatoes or allergic to English comfort food as well?" Dick added.

Ray chuckled. Harry glared at Dick. He was eyeing Felicity and felt Gary and she made a much nicer couple than her and the arrogant, smart-ass.

As they dined, Felicity mulled over Gary and Dick. They were about the same age. Dick looked older but was more handsome. Gary was more cute and easy to look at. Seating arrangement made it easy for Felicity to exchange glances with Dick. *He is so suave*, Felicity thought. Very well dressed.

She was sure he didn't have tattoos underneath that expensive suit and the way he ate. How he placed his napkin. Used the cutlery. Even drank the wine. Seemed so fine and classy to be the player type she avoided.

Dick remained composed through it all.

Felicity, what a knockout. Not a 10 but an 11. How could she not be married or spoken for?

Obviously related to social circles confining her. Even if she was an airhead, easily would have been a trophy wife for many he knew. Ray, her father, really full of surprises. Catching him off guard while he worked on his tan in Tampa Bay. Two weeks ahead of schedule on the latest job. Forcing him to return pronto to Montreal. This unexpected gorgeous creature which was his daughter. He couldn't wait to take Felicity out alone and talk to her.

"So, what's the verdict on the spuds?" Dick reiterated.

That ass, Harry thought.

Now the spotlight was on him again.

He was stalling shifting positions of the greens on his plate.

"Any condiments in it?" Harry asked.

"Just butter, salt, diced onions for flavour," May said.

"Onions?"

He knew it. He had to get out. He eschewed the stench of leeks. Last thing he needed was for them to learn more about his pernickety-ness around food.

"If he doesn't care for potatoes, let Harry sample your famous homemade vegetable soup?" Felicity suggested.

May was up and off towards the fridge

"Just take a few minutes to microwave and…"

"No, no, no. Listen, I've got to be going anyway."

Harry rose from his seat. It wasn't her imagination. Something was amiss. Harry could sense by the expression on May's face this was bad. He had to make up some excuse before he blew it with her.

"Just remembered something: I left the damned burner on my stove on."

"What?" May asked, incredulous.

"I had an instant cup of decaf before I left and just remembered I forgot to turn the burner element off."

"Better chauffeur him home full speed before his house burns to the ground," Dick said.

Ray laughed. Felicity and Gary noted Harry's angst.

"I'll get my car keys," May responded.

"No, the stove burner is just turned half-up."

"Then why bother? You can't miss dessert."

"On the other hand, you never know," Harry added.

May was stumped. What was wrong? This is bunk. She knew it. She knew he knew, she didn't buy it too.

"Harry…"

Harry scooped his photo album off the side table.

"Nice seeing you again, thank you for having me over."

Ray was smirking. He didn't know what triggered it, but hopefully his mother would now realise this old-timer was a ding-a-ling.

"I'm out."

Harry scooped his jacket off the chair moved very quick but fumbled with the locks trying to exit the front door.

May rushed after him.

"Harry, really what is it? What's wrong?"

He looked defeated. Glow in him gone. Like he did the last time she saw him when he lost her.

"Harry, please…"

"Don't be mad at me, May…"

"I'm not."

"I'll be in touch. Promise. Thanks for everything."

"Damn it," she said to herself.

It started so well. So dapper, trim, and neat.

He had pure white hair now but combed the same way.

What happened for him to go from romantic to suddenly at dinner the strange bird she recollected when she last saw him at Ogilvy's department store 49 years ago?

It was coming along so nice. Like wine aged so well.

The feeling of sweet innocence he evoked in her. Even though he was odd back then, she remembered he never had anything but soft feelings for her. Hoped in her heart they would have a chance again.

As Harry strode towards the busy street where he was going to catch a cab back to Dorval he thought, *I'm such an idiot, didn't even say goodbye. What a roller coaster.* High meeting May ruined trying to conceal his foodie bugaboos.

He heard something and stopped.

The municipality of Greenfield Park had planted trees along the boulevard. It was chirping from a bird. It couldn't be?

It looked like the same sparrow he'd photographed in Mont-Royal Park, sweet singsong chirping away.

An omen but good. Miss Picado's kindergarten class. Decades after losing her. Gary's idea to look up the few women he hardly ever knew that got away. The hell he was going to blow this break to meet May he fell into by fluke.

The scowls from her son who loathed him?

Too bad if Ray resented him. May, his flower of loveliness after all this time. He was going to war with his years of aloneness. The last chance in the last act of his life.

When May returned to the dining area, Ray and Dick were smirking. Gary chewing on food.

"He unwell?"

"I don't know what went wrong."

"Typical English," Ray snorted in French.

"Stop it," May shot back.

"You speak French, Gary?"

"No."

"Move here from Ontario," Ray asked.

"No, I'm from Vancouver," Gary answered.

"Vancouver!" Ray exclaimed.

"Yes," Gary added.

"Vancouver is a gorgeous city," Dick added.

"If girls were cities, Vancouver is you, Felicity," Gary added.

Everyone froze.

"Beautiful but very expensive to reside there," Dick said.

"Nature, mountains and ocean are free," Gary added.

Felicity was looking at Gary again.

"If B.C. is so beautiful, what are you doing in Quebec?" Ray demanded.

"A friend of mine in the military told me the best place to be poor in Canada is Montreal."

Everyone froze again.

"Not now. The government is cutting back," Dick said.

"Your English is very good," Gary added.

"My father is English and my mother is French."

"Two worlds," Ray added.

"Montreal is no place to be for a person unable to communicate in English and French," Dick said.

"Maybe Felicity could coach me?"

"Yes, I could teach you," Felicity exclaimed.

"You don't realise what you're up against," Dick added.

"What do you mean?"

"You don't stand a chance."

"Why?" Gary asked.

"Where were you educated?"

"I wasn't. I was in the Canadian Forces."

"While I majored in Law and Business Administration at McGill University," Dick added.

The wind stopped the idealistic sails of hope.

Ray grinned, relishing how pathetic Gary really was now.

"I better go. I might be late," Gary said.

"Late?" May asked.

"Yes."

"Late for what? You have to work?" Felicity asked.

"No, I don't have a job," Gary added.

"You don't have a job?" Her dad Ray repeated.

Painfully obvious now. Need anyone say more? Felicity felt crushed.

"But I hope to find one soon," Gary answered.

"He doesn't even have a job!" Ray exclaimed in French.

Ray looked at his mother. Under the table, May kicked Ray in the shins and he winced. Felicity considered that amusing and chuckled.

"Since you don't have a job, what do you do? How do you get around? How do you exist?" Ray demanded.

May glaring at him in response. Felicity went from smiling to hurt as she looked at Gary.

"I take the subway and the bus," he responded.

"He takes the subway and the bus!" Ray repeated to May and Felicity in French.

"I better go."

"Please, I want you to stay," Felicity said.

If Ray was a pit bull, he would have snarled.

"The system is on the holiday timetable. Bus to downtown only runs once an hour from Longueuil station."

"You're going to drive him," May ordered Ray.

"I'm not driving him home," Ray shot back in French.

"Then I'll do it myself," May fired back.

"I'll tag along for the ride," Felicity added in English.

This Gary blockhead was going to be more of a nuisance than Ray expected. He studied Gary a few seconds.

"How old are you?"

"32," Gary responded.

"And as you can see, he's different," Felicity added in Quebecois French.

"If a man is single and not married after 30, there's definitely something wrong with him," Ray said in French.

"Daddy, what do you know about the intricacy of human relations, you work in construction," Felicity expanded.

Gary wondered what they were saying about him in French.

"At least I have a job!" Ray shot back in English.

"And he's very competent. Overseeing more projects for me as well," Dick added in English.

"Your company's business is booming then?" May asked.

"Garelli Brothers are one of the most successful real estate developers in North America."

"They build skyscrapers, too, right?" Felicity asked.

"We have condominiums in the works all over the island of Montreal," Dick said.

"They're pretty influential," May added.

"And I hear supporters of the arts," Felicity said.

"They fund music festivals, symphonies, and dance all over the Eastern United States," Dick said.

"You obviously have connections?" May added.

"Absolutely," Dick answered.

"Maybe you could help Gary get a job," May asked.

Dick exchanged glances with Ray—who froze.

"What kinds of skills you have?" Dick asked.

"Paratrooper and pathfinder survival training," Gary answered.

"Even if you were versed in state-of-the-art laser weaponry, those aren't skills I'm seeking," Dick added, and Ray nodded.

"I'm good at following rules," Gary added.

"He could be a flunky," May added.

The grin disappeared off Ray's face.

"What did you do after the army?"

"I sold ice cream."

"Whereabouts and for how long?"

"In Winnipeg last summer. Pumped gas in Calgary. Worked at a car wash in Toronto."

"Any position of trust or responsibility?"

"Not outside the army."

Ray smiled.

"Someone has to give Gary a chance in Quebec," May said.

"Tell you what… I'll give you a job."

"You'll give me a job?" Gary asked.

Ray began to seethe anew.

"Limited experience translates to few bad habits."

"Thank you, thank you," Gary said with a smile.

Ray produced a business card and handed it to Gary.

"Come to my office Tuesday. We'll run you through some hoops. See what you're suited for and get you on a site."

Gary saw Felicity smiling. Her lovely, reassuring gaze comforted him. A high of happiness flowed through him.

He wished he knew her better so he could just hug her.

What in hell was his new boss doing, Ray thought.

Ray told May he couldn't drive Gary home because he had the 'runs'.

"Excuse me while I take a crap," Ray said in French and left the table promptly.

"Yea, more like verbal diarrhea," May retorted.

Felicity did the duty. May rode shotgun. Gary sat back.

After crossing over the St. Lawrence River, they were stuck in traffic chaos downtown following a Canadian hockey game. The Habs lost, and fans unleashed their frustration blaring horns and shaking fists at fellow motorists. It was stressing Felicity out so much she screamed as a car cut her off without signalling to zoom through an amber light.

"I can't deal with it anymore," she cried out, throwing her hands on her face. May exited the Mazda and they swapped places. Gary observed, bracing himself.

"Sorry about this," Felicity apologized.

"What's wrong?" Gary asked.

"It's painful for her to talk about," May said.

"Promise I won't say. I don't know anyone except Harry and my social worker in Quebec," Gary answered.

Another driver leaned on his horn and glared. He looked like a flesh-eating zombie foaming at the mouth.

"Go to hell!" May yelled out at him. Felicity looked at Gary in the rear-view.

She is so pretty I could just look at her and not even say anything for hours, Gary thought.

"Something that happened a long-time ago," May said.

"What?" Gary asked.

"I was in an accident when I was a little girl,"
Felicity looked at May to further explain.
"Speeding drivers who don't signal when they turn."
"Oh," Gary said.
"And I'm still not over it," Felicity said.
"It might be a good thing," Gary said.
Felicity and May exchanged baffled glances.
"How?" Felicity asked.
"Better you arrive 5 minutes late than speed and never arrive because you're dead," Gary said.
Felicity and May laughed.
"He's nice," May said to Felicity in French.
"Maybe even Mr. Perfect," she added.
Felicity glanced at Gary in the rear seat.
"What did you just say?" Gary asked May.
"That's private," May added.
"Was it hip?" Gary asked.
Felicity turned and smiled at Gary.
"It's a very nice thing," Felicity added, magnificently.

She is so amazing. Her smile and those big, beautiful, gentle eyes of hers. *What is happening? He never felt or this never happened in any other city,* he thought.

"Umm, does anyone know the time?" Gary asked.
Felicity glanced at her mobile phone.
"Almost 9 o' clock."
"Could you hurry?"
"Don't worry. It's a long weekend holiday," Felicity said.
"I have to tell you guys something."
"What's wrong," May asked.
"I go to bed at 9 o' clock every day," Gary said.
Felicity and May glanced at each other?
"Why?" Felicity asked.
"After 9 o' clock it's dangerous. Scary people out there."
"The nightlife in Montreal can be wild," May said in French.
"And be safer if party animals didn't get sloshed," Felicity added in French. May knew some side streets and was able to get onto Rue Notre Dame East. Zipping past the old port.

"I'm just past Pie-IX Street," Gary said.

May knew this area from back in the day. They were in the Old East End known as the French Ghetto in the old days.

She parked near well-kept apartment block. Eyed a few questionable young men loafing around the corner, conversing.

They were smoking. Probably up to no good.

"Would you like to come up and see my place?" Gary asked.

Felicity looked at her grandmother for a reaction.

"That okay?" Felicity asked her grandmother in French.

"He's harmless," May answered approvingly.

What a cute little place, Felicity thought as soon as Gary opened the door to his 1 and a half. The living room and kitchen were combined. A single, neatly made mattress with no bed legs was on the floor. They walked over to the window.

"This is my view."

"Nice, you can see skyscrapers downtown from here."

"Yes, and I can watch all kinds of people walking back and forth on the street," Gary said.

Felicity looked down. Hoodlum types were standing around, smoking.

"Can I offer you a glass of water?" Gary asked.

They sipped on water and watched gleaming lights of the Montreal skyline from afar. Felicity saw a notice attached to an appliance.

"What is that on your fridge?" Felicity asked.

Gary removed the magnetic reminder with felt pen writing on it from the fridge.

"My meal schedule."

Gary handed it to Felicity who read it aloud.

"Tuna fish with macaroni on Mondays.

Hamburger on Tuesdays. Soul food Wednesday and Thursday. Frozen fish and chips on Friday

Spaghetti on Saturday. Pizza on Sunday."

Felicity hesitated.

"And the Sweetest Day? What's this?"

"At the end of the month from the 29th on... If I have any welfare money left, I go for a treat."

"Once a month?" Felicity asked.

"Yes, if I don't go over budget."

"Something so fun only once?"

"Just until I find a job. Then I'll do it every weekend."

It made total sense but was bittersweet.

"Like to spend the Sweetest Day with me," Gary asked.

She looked at him. *She has such beautiful eyes,* he thought.

"I would love to," Felicity replied without hesitation.

Again, Gary couldn't believe it.

How lovely she was. How impossible it seemed her visiting him, to begin with.

"Oops, I remembered: It's 9 o' clock," Felicity added.

"Yes," Gary concurred.

He looked out below. Street people congregating laughed and jabbered. Gary recoiled from the view. Felicity saw fear manifest on his face.

"I'm gonna hide," Gary said.

"You're going to hide?" Felicity reiterated.

"Like I said, very dangerous after 9 o'clock. Scary people out there."

"I better be going," Felicity said.

He didn't live at home so wasn't a mama's boy.

Had no visible gadgets so wasn't a tech geek.

Was way too hesitant to be a player.

Doubted he was a gym rat covered in tattoos beneath his clothes or a bad boy in disguise either.

"Thanks for the water," she said.

"You're welcome," Gary answered.

Who was this Gary from English Canada?

How could a guy this soft have been in the army and war?

"See you on the Sweetest Day then," she said.

"Your number is in my phone. I'll call for sure."

Could he be her Mr. Perfect? Whatever she was feeling touched him too because Gary's heart skipped a few beats—

How could a girl this magnificent and sweet really be looking at me like this, he thought.

"Good night," Felicity said.

"Goodbye," Gary answered.

She could see feelings he was processing were stressing him, so she let herself out. Gary stared out the window. Watched Felicity and May drive off below. He looked at the skyline. The city felt more beautiful now.

*****

Gary lay on his floor mattress, musing and feeling.

'Yes', she said 'yes'.

Felicity was going to go out with him on the Sweetest Day.

It was the best 'yes' he had ever heard in his life.

Felicity's loveliness was a comforting and beautiful sensation.

If he could hug her, it would be like putting a bandage on a wound. Even heal dudgeon of doom pain.

I think I'm in love with her, he thought.

*****

Ballerina students, parents, and Nancy watched in awe as Felicity sailed and pirouetted airborne. Landed with grace. Extended her arms out and smiled. Everyone cheered. *What had so suddenly energized her,* Nancy thought.

She kept staring at Felicity with the same sense of awe as they closed up shop for the night.

"What?" Felicity asked.

"Yes? What?"

"What is going on with you?"

"Excited about the audition coming up?"

"More than that. Never seen you look so good."

Felicity gushed and grinned.

"You met someone!"

Felicity told her she met two hunks.

Both about the same age.
One was an executive her dad worked for.
He was confident, handsome, and well-off.
The other guy was an Anglophone from Vancouver.
Gentle. Respectful and cute.
"Describe the one your dad works for in one word."
"Hot," Felicity answered.
Nancy screamed.
"And the guy from B.C.?"
"Sweet," Felicity said.
Nancy screamed with delight again.
"Finally, finally! I'm so happy for you."

*****

It was not for debate, but the tension was palpable and heating up between May and her son since the Thanksgiving Day dinner.

"Can't expect me to stand and watch Felicity go for that English guy she met in the nut house who doesn't have a job."

"She's a grown woman capable of making her own choices."

"People don't move from British Columbia to Quebec! They go from Quebec to BC!"

"Canada is a free country," May answered.

"There is no winter in Vancouver! It just rains. No normal person would trade an umbrella and come here where it is dangerous freezing cold in Quebec!"

"She's your daughter—not your wife!"

"He's a successful big shot who went to McGill!"

"Felicity can decide for herself."

"She goes for that English guy and she'll go crazy too!"

"Forcing Felicity to do what you want is the crazy thing!"

"We know nothing about this guy from Vancouver."

When he was 10, he learned the truth. All the moaning and groaning. Creaking bed posts banging against the walls. Wishing one might be the daddy he never knew? Only thing these guys were ever interested in was 'wham-bam, thank you, Ma'am.'

Now was his daughter's time.

But she was different than her grandmother.

Felicity dated but was still pure.

Never lived in sin like his mother did.

He would not stand idle and watch his daughter ruin her life to fall for an unemployed mental case who couldn't even speak French when she had the chance to know a gentleman that could comfortably look after Felicity for the rest of her life.

Chapter 8

Harry stood outside a grocery store in his Dorval neighbourhood waiting. Hopefully, she wouldn't be too shocked about meeting him here, but this was the only way he could try to explain the reasoning for his abortive departure from Thanksgiving dinner.

His social faux pas drove a wedge between him and most people he ever knew. If she accepted this side of him, it would happen between them for sure.

When May pulled into the parking lot of the shopping plaza and saw him dapper in his pressed white suit, little black bow tie, brush cut pure white hair sticking straight up, holding flowers, a surge of joy swept through her being.

How can he still be so crazy about me? she wondered.

She stepped out of the car and continued to watch Harry waiting on her. She had not felt this kind of anticipation for decades. *How could this man be real? All this time—decades—single?*

"Hi."

The way Harry beamed, smiled, and looked at her touched her deeply.

"Hi," Harry returned.

She had never seen such an anticipatory expression of joy on any man the way Harry looked at her. How could he gaze on her with such ardour when she eclipsed her prime long ago?

What had happened to him all these years, she thought.

"Should have given you these many moons ago," Harry said as he handed May flowers and watched her close her eyes and inhale the nosegay of fragrances.

*****

As Harry pushed the buggy and they strode side by side, a realisation occurred to her where she was.

"P-P-P! The Picky People Place! What insanity! Who would shop here," May said.

"English West Islanders."

May glanced at the sparse products on shelves. Triple P specials were tagged on bags of white rice. Generic spaghetti. Plain tomato sauces with no added condiments.

"How does this business thrive in a world of foodie fusion!"

"They're comfort food specialists," Harry added.

May stopped. Harry too. The whole idea of this went against her grain.

"What's wrong?"

"Let's leave."

"Have a confession to make. I'm not an adventurous eater."

"This is it? The reason you left my dinner the other day?"

"Afraid so."

He didn't look so handsome anymore.

She couldn't comprehend it. Needed an explanation.

"I have a very sensitive palate."

"So do I and am able to appreciate the fine art of food and gastronomy even more!"

"Sorry."

May looked at him. Serious.

"It would make your social life smoother."

"What can I say? It is a handicap."

May loved gastronomy. Loved to cook. Adored cuisine.

More diverse the spices, better the sensation dancing on her palate.

Her and this oddball Harry? What a dumb idea.

"Sorry, but I don't think this is going to work."

Harry could see it in the expression on her face.

Whatever she felt for him had gone cold.

"May, please. I know I can be a bullhead SOB but…"

"What?" she added, fed up.

To deliberately deny oneself the joy of diverse culinary celebration. It was incomprehensible to her?

"You have no idea what you're missing."

"Wish I was able to appreciate food like you. I'd travel the world, pigging out on exotic grub every chance I got."

May considered his idea and stopped.

He had no pretence.

Knew who he was and what he stood for.

Was no phoney.

Would be nice to not be on guard around a man compared to the smooth operators she'd known in her day.

"You never did play games."

"I hope that's a plus."

"So is subtly."

"You'd like me more if I'd pretend and subtly lied?"

Harry got handsome again. He was as she remembered him.

Pathetic on occasion but always real and sincere.

"Do appreciate your forthrightness very much."

All was not lost. He still might yet experience love.

He did not want her to see the tears in his eyes and had to look away, pushing the buggy down the aisle.

"Forward on, to fresh, plain white bread," Harry added.

They stopped at the bread rack. May eyed it dubiously.

"This is it? White, Brown, and Rye?"

"Yes," Harry answered.

"Piss-poor selection."

Harry laughed.

"The Picky People white. To me, that's comforting."

Harry placed white bread in the buggy.

"Think we should experiment and go for the brown."

"May, there are two types of people in this world. People who like white bread and the people who like brown bread, and I'm a white bread kind of guy all the way."

How shallow. She shook her head, disgusted.

They passed rice, jars and cans of generic, plain sauces.

On generic shovelling. With generic labelling. Scribbled in generic black felt pen numbers. May stopped. Harry too.

"We miss something you want?"

"I didn't see spices."

"Salt and pepper are the only condiments at the P-P-P."

"You need to seriously listen up!"

Harry looked at her worried.

"Time for you to get adventurous and change."

It turned into a field trip. An hour later they were wandering around on Boulevard St. Laurent in an Asian vegetable emporium where May was in her element selecting brands of tofu. Harry accompanied her lugging a basket of tomatoes, green peppers, and an eggplant.

He wouldn't touch this stuff with a proverbial 10-foot pole.

May detected a look of dread on Harry's face as the cashier weighted and scanned the veggies.

"Grub for elephants and jungle beasts," Harry commented.

May smiled.

"You know this is going to be a problem with us."

"Yes, I'm sorry," Harry added.

"I enjoy food. Love to eat and savour everything."

"I know," he said, discouraged.

"Come over, and I can prepare some vegetable soup."

"I'd have to get pretty damn psyched up to do that."

"Let's start with an attempt?"

"Honestly, doubt I could handle the texture of all them veggies hitting my palate at once."

"Harry, this is not going to work?"

"Why not?"

"We're just mismatched."

"May, please don't judge me on my preference for food."

"Give me one good reason why?"

"I'll give you two."

"One: like you too much to care if it cost me double to eat separate meals each time we meet."

"You rich, Harry?"

"No, but two: I have more money than time to spend the dough I have left."

Harry schlepped the bags of vegetables and loaded them in the back of May's car. She was still not over that foray to the P.P.P. yet and was eyeing him sceptically.

"Not mad or disappointed in me, I hope," Harry added.

What a handsome devil he still was, she thought.

"No," she said with such softness, looking at him.

"No way you would have been able to dance around your eccentricities with food," she said.

"Right," he said with a smile.

What happened to Harry? He had a job. Was fit. For the most part well-adjusted. Was a catch. There must have been other women interested?

"Now, you know my worst flaw up front," Harry said.

Over years the many relationships with self-centred jerks. She had made her choice, and it was Big John who was a whip in the sack but a dullard when the whoopee was over.

If she only would have taken the time to go on a date with Harry to see what made him tick. She could see in the lost and lonely way he looked at her. There was pain, but it was sweet and sincere.

"Okay, guess If I prepared myself, I could try your veggie soup once," he said.

"Thank you," she said.

How madly Harry wanted to wrap his arms around her.

Her expressive emotional eyes glowed the way he remembered.

That was all she needed to take the lead.

May moved towards Harry, and they kissed.

The rush he felt was so high. So ineffable.

So sweet, he almost broke down.

Had he been waiting? Saving himself for her all this time. Not knowing it till now.

It was rush hour, and Harry told her to forget about driving back to the West Island in traffic. He watched her drive off. She came to a stop. Turned to glance at him out the window and wave and he returned the gesture.

*****

Harry had never been so damn happy in his whole life. He was on the verge of tears. In a trance on the 211 bus ride back to Dorval. He sat at the back where nobody could see him just in case he couldn't control himself if bawled like a baby. It had been too long. Way too long.

Just to be in her company. In her presence. By her side, shopping for an hour. He damn well knew what he was missing his whole life. *You, May,* he thought. *Your love.*

Years of loneliness had been alleviated with them embracing and that one long kiss. A gesture of affection natural for her, but for Harry monumental. Angels were singing in heaven.

God, what a hell of a sweet day, he thought.

*****

A gargantuan office tower.

Gary could see it from his east end bachelor suite.

Shimmered like a giant emerald glowing green at night.

He arrived 20 minutes early. Rode to the 15th floor. Hallways lined with mirrors and shiny silver trim. The door was locked when Gary tried to enter. Dick arrived coffee in hand, swinging his brief case, ten minutes tardy.

"Sorry, fender bender on the Decarie Expressway. Then an insane queue at a drive-through to get my caffeine fix."

*****

It was unlike any test Gary had ever taken.

Shapes. Circles. Squares. Rectangles. Triangles and arrows.

Backwards. Twisted. Turned inside out and upside down.

Reminded him of geometry, and he flunked that.

No reading comprehension. Not one single question about history, general knowledge, spelling, or vocabulary. How could he understand shapes he couldn't read? Gary sat gawking perplexed trying to get it for half an hour.

It was if the test was making mocking faces, calling him stupid itself. In the end, he randomly checked answers, guessing before time was up.

Gary sheepishly handed it to Dick.

"It was hard. Hope I did well enough to pass."

Dick glanced at the responses. All erroneous and he smirked. *Dumb ass,* he thought and suggested Gary take a break and return an hour later.

Gary wandered around a food court in a mall connected to the office tower above. He wanted but denied himself a coffee because it was 2 dollars and he needed that money to buy ground beef for two Spaghetti Saturdays.

Dick was leaning back on his leather chair, glancing back and forth between the test and at Gary fidgeting, nervously awaiting the results.

"How did I do?" Gary asked.

Insanely horrible, Dick thought but refrained from disclosing it.

"What's really relevant is your lack of job experience. Any explanation for that?"

"My social worker and psychiatrists say I'm disabled, but it's just feelings I have and take medication for that."

"Otherwise, you a pretty flexible guy?"

"Yes, I try to be."

"How long have you known Ray and his family?"

"Just a little while."

"Nice people, huh?"

"Yes."

"Ray tells me Felicity's an accomplished dancer?"

"And teaches kids' ballet class too," Gary said.

"So tell me, Gary, your relationship with Felicity serious?"

"Why?"

"Just curious. She seems like the real deal?"

"Yes. She's very pretty, talented, and sweet."

"What about sexually?"

Gary froze. "What do you mean?"

"You know."

"No, I don't."

Dick just stared.

Gary was trying to understand feelings going through him.

It was anger. Yes, he was angry.

"I'm talking in the sac?"

His words hurt.

Gary wanted to punch Dick in the face.

"You're going out with her? She's your girl? You are slamming her, right?"

A maelstrom of feelings boiled.

Gary wished Felicity was his girlfriend.

When Dick smirked, Gary would have liked to 'slam' Dick's face but instead pounded his fist on the desk.

"Whoa."

Dick spooked by Gary glaring at him now.

It was creepy.

The guy was psycho.

Who knows what this moron could be capable of if he snapped? He had to backpedal quick.

"Dude, you need to lighten up."

Gary continued to glare at him.

"I was just teasing."

"What you said is not funny."

"You were in the army and your resume also states you were in Afghanistan so I shouldn't be messing around like this."

"I was in the war, but I'm not a violent person."

"In this post-9/11 world, you never know."

"What you said about Felicity is unkind."

"You're a real gentleman. Protected a woman's honour all the way. Know what? It would be a pleasure to hire you."

Gary didn't flinch, move or blink.

In actuality, this was known as the 'blunt affect'.

A side effect of the anti-psychotic prescription medication Gary took, and it was freaking Dick out.

"Again, I apologize about inappropriate things, but you have to realise, people who work for me are an extension of myself. And if they can't handle a little pressure, well…"

Gary continued to stare, but his gaze was disarmed.

"I never thought of it like that," Gary added.

Dick rose from his seat.

"Call you tomorrow. Give you the address of a site."

Dick extended his hand. Gary shook it.

"That it?"

"Yes."

"I'm in?"

"Yup. You passed the stress test. You're hired."

"Thank you, thank you," Gary said.

After Gary left, Dick examined the spatial relations aptitude test. One. He got one right out of 40 questions.

Pathetic. Absolutely fucking pathetic.

IQ points weren't meted equitably.

They were determined by genetics.

This poor bastard could not be trusted to think for himself. Gary looked fit and had balls to eye fuck with him, but we're talking dumbest man alive.

How could a gorgeous, innocent, unsullied beauty, marriage material, quality woman like Felicity entertain dating a moron like this?

His foresight on how to play this should be safe.

Grunts on the job could bark orders at Gary for what to do.

And since all is fair in love and war, his actions were ethical to pre-empt and rescue that gorgeous ballet star Felicity from this hapless failure before it was too late.

Chapter 9

May underwent a series of medical tests and was informed to return and see the physician treating her immediately. The results were not good. At 86 years of age May accepted and was psychologically prepared to face death, but recently life changed meeting Harry again.

Ray customarily drove, but she had taken a taxi this time. The moment she arrived home, promptly telephoned Harry delighted to hear from her but he sensed something amiss.

"What is it? What's wrong?" Harry queried over the phone. Instead of replying May asked him another question.

"Ready to reconsider being adventurous?" she asked.

She tried to conceal distress yet he clued into the subtlest irregularity of inflection in her voice over the phone.

In the brief time she had come to know him again, there was no question there were moments of oddness, but he really was that sensitive a man too.

"What do you have in mind?"

"A picnic," May replied.

Harry was unready to experiment with food, but there was nothing more he wanted but to be in her presence again.

"I know a nice spot in Mont Royal Park."

She was feeling this because of him.

So many relationships over the years.

Good times but so many assholes too.

Never with someone like him.

A kind of man she never knew.

The way he looked at her like she was 21.

To be ill now.

Such rotten news, not only to her but unfair to him.

"Beaver Lake in Mount Royal Park. Can't wait to see you there, dear."

Harry was so overjoyed he couldn't sleep a wink.

Worried he'd look bedraggled but so high on the idea of getting close to May it didn't manifest at all.

How could this be happening, a second chance with her, in the end, 86 years of age?

May spotted Harry first. Dressed in his suit anew.

Sitting alone. Staring at sweethearts paddling rented rowboats on Beaver Lake.

When he saw May he rose.

She approached. No words.

If he would take her in his arms, she would gladly coalesce. To her completely natural and inevitable and he would have done so but isolated years left him crippled with the interpersonal life skills to do so.

"Hi," she said.

He was frozen. Transfixed. Just to look at her.

The utterance of her saying a simple 'Hi' magical.

"Hi," Harry tritely responded.

May instinctively sensed their bond. Vital to them both.

We are here. This is us. Time is short. Here and now.

They strolled on a trail past the towering oaks.

In a minute they were arm in arm.

A surge of joy imbued Harry.

What is this magic I am so suddenly feeling, he wondered?

If he were to petition the Gods to answer, Buddha would simply reply: it is love.

A bird zipped past them.

"See that! A real live bluebird."

"Yes, I did. That was really something."

"Usually see robins and sparrows around here."

She felt his naiveté was as cute as his bow tie.

"Why do you like birds so much?"

"Must have been one in my past life."

She never considered nature from that perspective before. Harry looked up. May followed his line of sight.

"Look at them. So harmless. Delicate and free."

"I'd like to catch one and pet their tiny little heads," May added.

Harry fumbled through his windbreaker pockets.

"What are you doing?"

It was the same sparrow following him around.

He had seen it here on Mount Royal and in May's residential Greenfield Park neighbourhood last week.

Harry snapped a few shots.

Two of them, chirping and chasing each other in circles.

"I know that bird!"

May chuckled. Looked up and then back at him.

"Harry?"

"Yes," he said still snapping photos.

"Those birds are in love."

Harry lowered his camera and looked at her.

They stopped under the large oak tree.

Spread out a blanket and shared some wine in paper cups.

When she produced a pickled delicacy and bit into it savouring the flavour, Harry cringed, thought, *Yuck—stinky food.*

"Mont Royal was a nice touch. The birds. Fall foliage leaves. Trees above," May said.

Still, Harry saw something, doubt. A look of dismay. Dread.

No way a woman he longed for should feel this way.

Not if he could help it.

"I'm going to ask you again? What's wrong?"

"What do you mean?" May answered.

"Same thing I asked you about yesterday on the phone?"

She looked at him poker-faced.

"Please, I'm all ears. Whatever it is."

Harry picked up on the slight tinge of tears in her eyes.

"Please," he urged her.

She had to face facts.

86. Terminally ill.

Made it all the more important they were here.

Meantime Harry thought, *she doesn't want me. Doesn't have the heart to voice it.*

Harry could not look at her.

The expression on her face pained him.

She knew he didn't have experience in these matters so here it goes, looking at him dead serious with dread.

Harry looking back, stunned.

"I'm sick. Doctors say my heart could give any moment."

"Doesn't matter. I miss you, May. Want it to be like when we were kids. Like when I lost you at Ogilvy's department store the 2nd time all those years ago," Harry replied.

It took a moment to compose herself to respond.

"Well, how about this? The answer is, yes.

Yes, Harry. I want you, and I need you."

He threw his arms around May.

She hugged him tight.

She cupped Harry's face into her hands.

Inside, Harry soared with joy.

"Yes." He had found her. She was breathless.

They had caught the old-time magic once again.

With exception of glances on the drive to Harry's West Island bungalow, they were silent.

Recovering from how unbelievably wonderful it felt.

May pulled up in front of Harry's little house a half hour later.

"Now I only have one concern?"

"Anything?" Harry replied.

"No more shopping at the PPP."

"For you, yes."

They kissed. As awkward as 13-year-old sweethearts.

"Sorry," Harry added.

She laughed.

"Out of practice when it comes to smooching," he said.

She kissed him slow and soft on the lips.

"There is not one thing wrong with that in the world."

Harry was floating.

How was he going to contain himself?

These fantastic feelings of elation he was experiencing.

He reached into his pocket. Produced a pack of candy.

"Since we skipped dessert, may I offer you a jujube?"

"That would be nice," May said with a smile.
"What's your poison?" Harry asked.
"Cherry red," May said smiling.
Harry shuffled the pack.
Yellow, green, and red jujubes fell into her palm.
"There you go, dear."
Harry watched May sample the candy in awe.
"What?" she asked.
He was still in a daze from the miracle of it.
To encounter the love of his life after so many years.
"How could you still be so beautiful after so many moons," he told her.
How could he think that?
None of it mattered. All those men.
Where she'd been. Who she'd been with?
What he felt for her was real.
Pure. Unconditional. And she didn't deserve it.
"Come here," she said.
Harry fell in her arms.
They kissed again.
My God, May thought as she held Harry close.
I have never felt this feeling my whole life.
His kiss more surging with feeling than any bodily erogenous zone she could recollect.
A pure sweet spot.
Now, this was first love.
And she was hooked.
If Harry could die now the endless wait to hold May would have been worth it.
Why had he been deprived of this joy so long?
This connection he longed for his whole life.
"I'm never going to let you go. You hear that?" he said.
She held him close.
What a beautiful man, she thought.
May would have made love to Harry but could sense the encounter had overwhelmed and been too much for him.
When it was over Harry watched her drive off.
86 years old.

He had never been so happy in his whole life.
He was born again.

*****

Ray met Dick, and they ascended the caged construction elevator in the latest glass, high-rise condo to dot the Montreal skyline.

"Looking good. Looking good," Ray said glancing about.

"My guys are just adding finishing touches. Tradesmen will inspect it next. Should be ready Thursday."

"Damn, you did it again."

"Thanks. Anything else?"

"Something I'd like to discuss but it may not really be any of my business."

"What?" Ray asked wondering.

"I hired your daughter's boyfriend."

"The guy I met at your Thanksgiving soiree."

Ray grinned.

His hunch was right.

The big shot has the hots for his daughter.

"Felicity has never had a steady boyfriend in her life."

Dick looked at Ray, incredulous.

"And as far as that Gary guy from English Canada goes, I don't see any future for them at all."

Fantastic, Dick thought.

He had to make his move.

"Just wanted to mention he won't be joining our team on the next downtown project going up."

"Personally, I don't give a crap. My mother was hoping you'd give him a job."

"He took a test. Only thing I can offer him is an unskilled labourer position on a townhouse complex we're developing in Île Bizard."

"Your business decisions have nothing to do with me."

"I'm relieved it's not an issue."

"Like I said, as far as I'm concerned, this Bubblehead is totally wrong for her and she'll figure that out soon."

"Took the liberty of Googling Felicity.

She is one of the finest and most promising ballet dancers in the country. When I learned of Gary's results, I was concerned."

"Appreciate that," Ray added with a smile.

"Unexpected to uncover something of this nature…"

Ray stopped. *Perfect. He wants her. He likes Felicity.*

"Invite your daughter to the opening this weekend?"

Ray smiled.

"You want to get to know Felicity?"

"Would love the chance to meet and get better acquainted with her."

They shook hands.

He knew it.

He had seen the effect Felicity had on men many times.

She was a knockout.

With Dick in the picture, it was finally going to pay off.

May was a social butterfly all her life, so Ray knew something was amiss when she declined to accompany them to the opening of the new downtown office tower on the weekend. Daily routines were same but these motions were never perfunctorily performed like now. She was very distracted by something? Prior to them leaving Saturday night watched her aimlessly clicking through TV channels.

Maybe this is a good thing, Ray thought.

She won't be able to meddle with the idea of matching his new boss and daughter now.

While Ray regaled construction trade anecdotes to Garelli Executives from the U.S. Dick used the opportunity to approach Felicity by herself sipping champagne in a corner.

"Your father is a wiz at what he does."

"Your opportunity made him very happy."

"If you can run a business, provide exceptional service, and make people smile in this competitive, cruel world, it is all the more rewarding."

Felicity flashed a million dollar smile at him.

Wow, what a babe, he thought.

She's prettier than New York models he's dated.

"Incidentally, I hired your friend Gary for a job."

Felicity's eyes lit up.

"Terrific!" she shouted out.

Is she ever gorgeous! Dick thought but was infuriated she was pleased.

"It's not much. Just a temporary construction labour position."

"Gary is going to be so happy."

Felicity looked at Dick. "Thank you," she said.

Her gratitude was sincere.

This really pissed him off.

"Listen, I wanted to have a few words with you about Gary. He seems rather unsure of himself."

"Oh, that's because he doesn't speak French and has had trouble finding friends."

"You two close?"

"He's a very nice guy."

"You going out?"

"Depends on your definition of 'going out'?"

"You tell me?"

"I can tell you I've been to his place and think he's very sweet."

Shit, Dick thought.

"If you don't mind me asking, how long have you been seeing each other?"

Felicity paused. *Does he? Does he really like me?*

"A little while?"

"So, in other words, you just met?"

"Yes. Why do you ask?"

"Well, I was entertaining the notion if you're not officially seeing him, perhaps we could have lunch?"

"Lunch?"

He does. This super-hot guy likes me, and he could have any woman he wants.

"Yes, lunch. A little harmless lunch."

"That is, unless Gary is the jealous type."

Felicity considered this.

It wasn't fair to Gary to accept but then again, rich handsome hunks don't exactly ask her out.

"No, he's not like that at all."

"Then we're on," Dick announced.

*****

Gary took the ride out to Île Bizard section of Montreal the evening before. He wanted to ensure he wouldn't be late tomorrow morning and knew exactly where to disembark the bus. Luckily welfare paid for his Metro transit pass covering the cost of all rides on buses and subways in the Urban Community.

It would have been impossible to get this job if they did not. When he arrived the next morning at 7 a.m. Rock n' Roll music was blaring while carpenters, labourers, and tradesmen did their thing. Ones under contract by the Garelli Brothers wore matching blue hard hats, pants, and shirts.

A French Canadian Flunky who worked with a cigarette constantly dangling from his mouth, gestured at Gary to move extraneous debris into waste bins located at the edge of the townhouse site. Gary had been to and fro for 3 hours when a garbage truck slowly pulled up.

His first thought was did they find him?

Did the garbage men track me down?

If so, how could that be?

Least it wasn't a Montreal Urban Community trash truck.

Instead of 'GO GREEN' it read 'Ronnies Rubbish Removal'. It didn't matter.

His heart began to pound like mad. He dropped the shards of dry wall he was lugging and dashed off to hide in a townhouse with no tradesmen working inside.

The same instant the French flunkie stepped out of the portable toilet after taking a crap.

"What ta fuck!" he yelled out in French.

He ran into the empty townhouse to chase down the dogger and saw Gary crouched in a corner, shaking.

Immediately he began yelling in French.

"What is wrong? Get your ass to work."

Gary heard bins emptying into the garbage truck and being compressed. Noise making him jump with every crunch.

"Now! Get your ass in gear and stop dogging it!"

Gary was shaking. Wet—sweating like a pig.

The French Flucky suddenly realised what was up.

"You drunk? You high?

You're a fucking doper, aren't you!"

He yelled and screamed for minutes.

Only time Gary understood a word of the bellowing was when the English word 'fuck' was mixed in the middle of all the epithets. Gary heard beeping—meaning the garbage truck was backing out and leaving the site.

"Useless as tits on a bull!"

The flunky spat a big green booger towards him that luckily missed and Gary bolted. Carpenters on rooftops witnessed him running full out towards the porta-potties and laughed, thinking that dude has to take one big shit.

Gary consumed a large granola breakfast so he would have lots of energy to work hard his 1st day, but it was all for naught when he opened the portable potty door and puked. French flunky reported it to the site supervisor complaining this English guy they hired was another dope fiend.

For the safety of tradesmen, the supervisor relegated Gary to cleaning the portable potty toilets the rest of the afternoon. By the end of the shift, all the workers on site heard about this new English guy's crazy day.

The supervisor advised Gary that if he wanted to return tomorrow, he was going to have to pee in a bottle so his urine could be analysed for drugs.

Gary had never experimented with cocaine or marijuana in his life. Only drugs he ever ingested were anti-psychotic medication to suppress panic attacks. Gary waited for the bus home after work when a minivan pulled up packed with bi-lingual French-Canadian Laborers.

He overheard them chat and knew they understood English.

"Yo, Gary. You wanna come with us to the bar?"

"I don't drink," Gary replied.

The labourers glanced at each other incredulously.

"Why not?" Another labourer demanded to know.

The reason Gary avoided alcohol was because it was verboten to consume with anti-psychotic medication prescribed to him, but he couldn't explain this to them.

"I like the taste of Coca-Cola and Pepsi better,"

Gary answered.

French labourer guys laughed.

"C'mon with us anyway."

"Yea, we're going to see titties," another labourer leered.

"I don't do that either," Gary answered.

Some laughed. Others were stunned.

"You a fag or something?" Another voice called out.

Gary looked. They were all staring, eagerly waiting for an explanation.

"Watching strippers is like someone waving a piece of chocolate cake in front of you saying, 'Mmmm, looks good, huh? Too bad you can't have any'."

The whole van exploded with guffaws, and Gary could hear them howling as the van burned rubber, speeding away.

*****

Juan spearheaded a New York City Ballet company searching for talent in this year's rendition of 'The Nutcracker' held at Place-Des-Arts in Montreal.

Dancers from Victoria B.C. to St. John's, Newfoundland, journeyed to vie for the opportunity because of his reputation for discovering talent that emerged to be stars on Broadway.

During the week, Juan appraised various dancers dictating verbal notes into a compact cassette recorder while an assistant captured their missteps or finesse on digital film.

Four finalists were selected. Their identities anonymous till the very end. Felicity was the last candidate being ranked.

Juan gazed at her moving slow, graceful, beautiful, airborne, landing with a spinning pirouette, arms shooting skyward synonymous of a visual exclamation mark!

Felicity took a quick bow and exited stage left.

Juan noted her curriculum vitae stated she was under Hanna Burnbaum's tutelage. Had been a student of hers since she was 6 years of age.

Felicity's technique was magnificently eclectic.

Compared to the other candidates, he felt Felicity's technique was refreshing. Her energy unbridled. Her style uniquely contemporary.

An instructor at Hanna's academy as well.

Hometown dancer. Also an advantage.

Juan glanced across the auditorium at Hanna seated on the right. His first time in Montreal but this was how the game was played worldwide. Felicity was the hometown star. Montreal's ace card out in the open for him to see now.

*****

Nanna and Daddy were arguing when Felicity arrived home. Since Thanksgiving, they had been at it incessantly.

She thought it was cute, but her daddy loathed the idea of her Nanna and Harry dating. When their words became vicious Felicity put on earphones and listened to sweet love songs.

"What are people going to think?"

"I don't care!"

"They're going to think it's disgusting!"

"That's their problem."

"You're disgracing the memory of John!"

"John was not your real father."

"This smorgasbord of men has to stop!"

"Never!"

"Does he know who you are?"

"What?"

"You know exactly what I'm talking about!"

"No, I don't."

"That you're easy."
"I'm am not."
"You disgust me."
"I carried you 9 months!"
"You disgraced us both!"
"I'm your mother!"
"He wants to lay you like the rest!"
"You're wrong about him!"
"I'm not!"
"Harry loves me!"
Ray mockingly laughed.
"Pathetic."
"I am dying!"
May scampered off, slamming her bedroom door shut.

Never had he heard his mother weep like this and it cut deep.

Harry's fault. She turned her from bra-burning feminist into a sentimental schoolgirl. She must be very sick. Probably cancer?

And she was right.

What an ungrateful ass he was uttering such vicious words to the woman that gave him life. How could she fall for that old English guy Harry like this at the end?

Chapter 10

From inside the Outremont Ballet Academy, Nancy watched a candy apple Vette pull up and park.

When Dick stepped out, decked in suit and tie.

Slicked back hair, tan, removed his shades and black racing gloves, she screamed.

Felicity was applying touches of makeup in the alcove.

"He is gorgeous!" Nancy called out.

Dick entered. "Hello there?"

The guy's a damn, movie star, Nancy thought.

"Hi," Nancy said.

"You chum around with Felicity, I assume?"

"My partner in crime will be out shortly."

Felicity hurried around the corner and appeared.

"Hi."

"Hello, my dear."

"You're early?"

"Cancelled my afternoon appointments."

"Why?"

"So I spend more time with you."

Felicity blushed.

Nancy turned to look at Felicity.

Threw her hand over her heart.

Closed her eyes and mouthed the words: "WOW."

It was an exceptionally balmy afternoon so they dined alfresco at a Bistro in the Latin Quarter. On the a la carte menu Dick chose the free-range grilled beef and breaded cucumbers. Felicity a chicken breast marinated with Creole spices and Cesar's salad.

The headwaiter presented a magnum with distinguished red-lettered labelling.

"The baby ice wine request, sir."
"Wait a second. We shouldn't be drinking that.
It's way too expensive. I'll just have a piña colada."
Dick motioned the waiter to continue.
He popped the cap and deftly poured the wine.
"This is too much."
The headwaiter smiled.
"Why not? You deserve the best."
The waiter smiled.
"Enjoy," he added and exited.
They toasted and drank.
"Well?"
Felicity contemplated the flavour.
"Superb," she replied.
"It's from British Columbia.
Has to be 8 degrees below Celsius before they can harvest the grapes."
While Felicity sipped on the ice wine, Dick produced a small package and placed it in front of Felicity.
"Whoa, now? Wait a second!"
"You're a special woman, Felicity."
She was embarrassed and flattered.
He was going all out.
Felicity stared at the small package on the table in front of her. Did he really like her that much?
"Open it."
Felicity took out a bracelet with little ballerina slippers, dangling from it, made from gold.
She was stunned.
It was the nicest little surprise gift she had ever received.
"I can't accept this…"
Dick smiled.
He sure is nice-looking, Felicity thought.
"Why are you doing this?"
"Gary can't afford to treat you like this so, why not?"
Why is he being so nice, Felicity wondered.
"Let me help you."
Dick placed the bracelet around Felicity's wrist.

"This is the kind of treatment you get when you go out with a guy who's successful and knows where he's going in life."

Felicity looked at the bracelet dangling from her wrist.

The gold glistened.

"Don't you have a girlfriend?"

"No."

"I can't believe you're not married."

"I'll be honest. There's been lots of women. But they didn't care, they just wanted…" Dick checked himself.

Better not poison her mind.

"I don't get it? Where do I fit in," Felicity asked.

"Wanted our first date to be memorable. I'm single. You're semi-single. Timing in our lives seems right."

It was too good to be true.

She was utterly mystified.

This rich, handsome man was going for her?

"Listen, it's been fabulous. The food. The wine. Your gift."

Dick stared and grinned.

"My hunch is you're not impressed?"

"Hate to seem ungrateful but…"

"I knew it. It's why I admire you," he said.

Felicity glanced away.

Dick's gently directed her face to look at him.

"Why do you live with your father and grandmother?"

"Uncertainty of performing arts means no steady pay."

"That all you really want. To dance?"

"It's been my dream since I was six years old."

Dick rested his hand upon hers.

"If you were my girl, I'd take care of you."

Felicity gasped.

If overlooked for the Nutcracker he would save and rescue her. Could he be Mr. Perfect?

*****

Ms. Jepson eagerly waited to hear how an Anglophone Man with mental illness obtained employment without her intervention in predominately Francophone Montreal.

As usual, Gary was clean. Well groomed. Polite.

He explained he met a woman at the psychiatric unit in the hospital whose dad worked for a guy that gave him a job.

He told her it was terrible until he peed in a cup and the rest of the week went excellent.

"What happened?"

He didn't want to disclose that information.

"Why?" he asked.

"Please, Jarry?"

Gary encountered hostile individuals in Afghanistan and living in low-income communities travelling through provinces. Ms. Jepson was the first person he met on his journey across Canada that was kind to him.

"I saw them."

"Who?"

"The garbage men."

"What did you do?"

"I ran. Went to hide."

Most of her clients never made it this far.

How did this delicate man keep a job in the rough and tumble construction trades an entire week?

Perhaps he was not mentally ill as diagnosed but simply misunderstood?

"The 1st week on the job for a person with a psychological disability is highly, highly stressful."

Gary looked at her.

"I'm very proud of you, Jarry."

Even though she was heavy and not pretty, he wanted to hug her.

*****

This was it.

The Sweetest Day.

In February early as the 28th.

In refreshing spring, sultry summer, romantic fall and winter, 29th, 30th or 31st.

Not that Montreal allocated more funds for social services than other places, but being more budget-friendly enabled Gary to glean more leftover welfare money than in other cities.

He had a lucky 13.00 dollars left and was going to meet Felicity for a date. The bus ascended, winding roundabout Ave De Pins, stopping in the Mount Royal Park public parking lot.

He stepped off. Saw her immediately.

Watched her for a few moments.

He had lived in many cities and never come close to encountering anything like her.

How could such a sweet and beautiful girl like that be standing there—waiting for him?

Felicity smiled. *There he is,* she thought.

Always with his knapsack. Shoulders slouched.

Lost looking. But cute. Resolute, kind, and dependable.

It drizzled. Droplets expanded. Then started to pour.

"This way!" Gary shouted.

They ran off like kids. Stopped under a giant oak.

Some mega-sized leaves that hadn't shed, shielding them from moisture. Felicity sneezed.

"Bless you," Gary returned.

"Thanks," she said, smiling back.

He is so fine, she thought.

They glanced up.

"Few clouds passing. In a few minutes, it will clear."

Gary saw the little hairs on Felicity's arms sticking up.

Even they were beautiful.

"You're cold?"

"I wasn't prepared for rain."

Gary dug through his knapsack.

Pulled out an umbrella.

Clicked it open completely shielding them from the shower.

"Lucky I'm from Vancouver," he said.

Felicity was still shivering.

"What do you have in there?" she asked.

"Toque. Gloves. My cell. Medication. This…" Gary handed Felicity a black sweater.

"You must have been a boy scout?"

"No, just the army."

She slipped the sweater on and smiled.

"Thanks, now I'm warm."

Even in a boring sweater, she is so lovely, he thought.

"You're just perfectly made."

"Ballet training."

Gary looked at her.

"Pretty as an angel. You can't train for that."

Felicity could tell he really meant it.

Would have kissed him right there but the rain stopped, and he clicked close the umbrella.

"Hurry before it starts again!"

Autumn sunlight seeped between clouds floating by.

Wind velocity high but moments of calm between as well. Dew drops reflected on grass.

Felicity and Gary walked by Beaver Lake.

Exchanging glances.

Lost in each other's eyes.

Gary dreamed about touching her.

The contours and soft creases of her face.

The city assembled a makeshift playground that was becoming a popular spot before it became too cold.

Teens were throwing a football.

Children were playing tag.

Gary pushed Felicity and kids on a merry-go-round.

Round and round. Circles and circles.

The child in Felicity had come out, and she was loving it. When that was over, they ambled over to the swings where he pushed Felicity once.

Twice. Three times.

Felicity laughed away.

"When was the last time you were on a swing?"

"Years!" Felicity called out.

After a few more pushes he caught her from behind and spun Felicity in circles.

When the momentum stopped, Gary stared at her.

Now, kiss me, she thought as she looked at him, smiling.

Gary wanted to but hesitated

"Let's go!" Gary said.

It was the perfect moment, and Felicity was disappointed.

As they strolled along the park path again, he could sense something wrong.

He had minded his manners.

Thought he behaved appropriately yet was unable to understand exactly what was wrong.

Felicity discerned the unease.

Okay, so he didn't make his move.

At least I know for sure he's not another Don Juan.

The sun began to recede, and they were sitting on a spread-out blanket beneath a large deciduous, tree shedding leaves.

He was staring up.

"Look," Gary said.

She followed his train of sight.

Tiny propeller bits, swaying back and forth landing on the ground amidst golden foliage of leaves.

"Wonder what they are?" Felicity asked.

Gary knew from loaning library books since he could not afford to buy them.

"Long-winged keys from maple syrup trees."

Felicity suddenly heard a peculiar noise.

"What is that?" she interjected.

Felicity could hear a clicking sound.

Gary pointed off.

"Mr. Woodpecker hacking away," Gary answered.

Felicity saw the bird and laughed.

"There!" Gary pointed and shot out.

A squirrel jumped from tree-to-tree.

Gary produced leftover popcorn from his knapsack and was now waving it at the squirrel, but it scampered off.

Felicity spotted another park creature frolicking about. "Look!"

Gary saw it, trying to entice it with the treat in his hand. "Come here. Come on."

A pip-squeak scampered down a tree.

Gary fed it a popcorn kernel.

While it munched, Felicity and Gary noticed the woodpecker stopped. Was looking over and observing them all.

"Felicity, I'd like you to meet Mr. Woodpecker and Mr. Pip-squeak."

"Hi, guys."

Gary held out a single kernel.

This time the pip-squeak took it right from his hand.

They watched the pip-squeak watching them while it munched and crunched.

"The same nibbling sound we make when we eat at the popcorn at the movies," Gary added for commentary.

Felicity's laugh startled the pip-squeak, and it scampered off, back up a tree.

Felicity tilted her head against Gary's shoulder.

He looked at her.

She smiled.

God, she is so beautiful, he thought.

Now, do it. Kiss me, she thought.

He wanted to kiss her again but felt tentative.

He had never been in a similar situation so was still uncertain and didn't want to ruin this Sweetest Day if he was wrong?

Instead of being disappointed this time she pointed up. "There he goes…"

"What a life, jumping from tree-to-tree all day. Only worry about foraging food. Wish I was a pip-squeak," Gary said.

Felicity giggled.

How was she going to deal with this?

She wanted him, but it was going to take time.

Birds began to sing overhead.

Gary looked up in awe.

"Like it here, ha?" Felicity asked.

"Love it," Gary replied.

"Listen." Birds going, tweak, tweak.

They paused.

Water trickled nearby.

"Sound of a stream," he said.

"Pretty," she said.

A little girl in a pink dress grinned at them.

"Kid smiles."

The little girl skipped towards her family.

Felicity looked up at trees.

"Imagine if trees could talk?"

"They do. Tell me stuff every Sweetest Day," Gary said.

"What do they say?"

"Best things in life are free. Or under a 1.99," Gary said.

She felt like taking Gary and making the first move, but a raccoon materialised and she screamed.

Gary tossed his remaining popcorn.

The raccoon snatched kernels and scampered off.

Felicity laughed.

"Finally, I say a prayer," Garry added.

Gary lay down on the blanket looking up.

Felicity same beside him too, looking up at the trees.

"Thank you, God, for big, tall trees that tower over and protect us. Thank you, God, for letting my ears work we so

I can hear the birds singing...

Thank you, God, for letting my eyes work so I can see the big blue sky and white puffy clouds moving with the wind. And thank you, God, for letting me live so I don't have to feel the pain I did when I was in the war."

Gary sat up.

Felicity followed and looked at him.

"Having fun," he asked.

She didn't even know him a month ago?

Who is he?

Why did it take so long?

He is rare. Boyfriend material, she thought.

"I love it here," Felicity said.

La Banquise was a 24-hour, Montreal French Fries and Poutine gastronomic institution.

It was pouring rain outside now and loaded.

Everyone ate here.

Students. Business men.

Starving artists. Drug addicts.

Felicity and Gary sat in single seats.

Rock n' Roll was reverberating.

Gary ordered the large size basket that came with two pops and unlimited refills.

"Ready for the 1st one?" Gary.

"Yes," Felicity replied.

Gary fed her the 1st fry.

It was dangling, dripping with gooey gravy.

"Ummm," she moaned as she closed her eyes and savoured it.

"You've got to chew it very slowly.

Let each bite roll around your mouth for 10 seconds before swallowing."

This was the first time Gary actually thought Felicity was hot. So sexy watching her consume one poutine covered fry moaning with bliss as she indulged. During the meal, Felicity also fed Gary fries.

They took turns doing this, laughing and giggling at how ridiculous it was minus saying much except when taking breaks from gorging out, sipping on their soda pop, fountain drinks.

"My nanna would love it here," Felicity said.

"Any hidden places you know about?"

"What kind of food do you like?"

"Chicken," Gary said.

"Bar-B-Barn. Best chicken in town.

Guy and St. Catherine Street downtown," she said.

"Can't wait to have soul food there," Gary commented.

He wanted to ask Felicity to accompany him too.

She would have said yes but he restrained himself, and again she felt dejected.

"Excuse me while I go to the ladies room."

She walked away.

As she approached the table 5 minutes later saw the discouraged look on Gary's face. All it took was for her to smile and joy instantly surged in him again.

From La Banquise they headed to St. Denis Street.

Plateau Montreal's bohemian restaurant, bar, and café district. Rain stopped and streets shined.

Couples, students, and goths sashayed about.

She dinned in the area yesterday with Dick and felt a pang of regret.

She should have refused to go out with Dick, but after dating so many bad boys and players, couldn't resist his assurance, smile, and selfless largess.

Dick disclosed knowing many females.

Women threw themselves at him.

He could pick any lady he wanted and chose her.

What more affirmation she was special than that?

Gary was a struggling, independent loner.

He and Dick were anything but from the same world.

Damn it, why did they both enter her life the same time?

They came to a stop in front of a café 'Aux Deux Marie'.

"My favourite place to go for a sweet," Gary added.

Felicity and Gary contemplated a melange of delectable desserts behind glass.

The counter girl stood watching them.

It was the first time she saw Gary in the company of a woman. He had been around a few months.

She had told him in broken English she had a boyfriend. Almost called the police for fear of him stalking her as he persisted to awkwardly attempt to make conversation and lingered around the premises indecisively.

Felt sad when she learned why.

"Time again?" counter girl enunciated in broken English.

"Yes, but you know how it is. I have to make my decision very carefully because I can only afford to come here once a month."

Gary glanced at Felicity.

"Which one you fancy?"

Felicity was stunned.

So many choices.

Impossible to choose.

"Let's see? Oreo cookie cream. Old-fashioned apple pie. Banana chocolate chip. Strawberry cheesecake. Mocha Fudge. Hopscotch buttercream. I'm overwhelmed."

"That a good thing or a bad thing?" Gary asked.

"I want to gobble them all up."

Gary would have loved that.

Hoped she would come here with him and try every pie every Sweetest Day.

He pointed to one she didn't mention.

"How about this? One of the best of the best."

"Chocolate Mouse Royale?"

Felicity smiled.

Gary and Felicity bent to study it behind the glass.

Hues of brown, dark, and milk chocolate icing made it diabolically delectable, blowing the calorie count number into the heavens.

"Yes, that one."

Gary carefully sorted and counted out the last of his welfare money savings. Assorted loonies, quarters, and dimes. The counter girl noticed he only had 5 cents, one nickel left.

Felicity relished in delight, feeding each other delectable pieces of Chocolate Mousse Royale.

She fed him the penultimate chuck and giggled.

"You have fudge on your cheek."

Felicity used her finger to gently wipe it from his face and sucked it off her index finger.

Now, Gary thought, *is she sexy, beautiful, and sweet.*

"So this is what you do on your special day?

Go to Mont Royal Park to feed pip-squeaks.

Visit La Banquise to have French Fries dripped in poutine, then come here to Aux Deux Marie to go for a high quality sweet?"

"Yes."

Gary fed Felicity the last piece of Mousse Royal.

Felicity moaned and added in French, "Magnificent."

"How was your experience?" he asked.

"Ecstasy," she said.

He loved that she loved it.

"Lastly, I say my Sweetest Day end of grace:"

"Thank you, God, for giving the pastry chefs talent and power to make such sweet fluff…"

And thank you, God, for bringing me this sweet girl,

Gary thought, looking at her.

Felicity gazed at him.

She had never been on a date like this.

"And you do this all alone?"

"Yes," Gary replied.

"Don't you have any army acquaintances in Montreal?"

"Yes, some pals from basic training were wounded in action. I searched and found one but he was dead."

"You still know Harry and others from the hospital?"

"I don't know them very well."

"That doesn't matter anymore."

"Why?"

"Two reasons."

Gary looked at her.

"One: You are your own best friend."

"I am my own best friend?"

That possible? True? Maybe, Gary thought.

He had survived like this a long time but now wanted her to be with him.

"And two,"

Felicity took Gary's hand.

"Now, you know me."

It was drizzling again.

Felicity was holding his hand. Gary looking at her.

Outside, the wind blew hard against the building.

"Listen?"

Rain drops pinged against the glass.

Felicity closed her eyes and tuned into the sound.

"Neat, huh," Gary asked.

Felicity opened her eyes.

The gentle sound of pings against the window punctuated the silence.

She wanted him.

"Ohhh… romantic rain. So nice…" she said.

They left when the drops and the gentle sound of rain against the window stopped. There was nothing to say. She had taken him by the hand and then walked. The feelings within him were so overwhelming he wanted to run and at the same time merge as close to her as possible. Just like they were boyfriend and girlfriend.

Felicity's loveliness petrified him.

He was feeling what he never felt before.

A happiness. He had never been this happy his whole life?

"May I offer a suggestion?"

He would do anything to prolong the moment with her.

"Sure."

"Swear you won't be offended?"

"Cross my heart," Gary answered.

They stopped.

Turned to face a store display window.

"What is it?" he asked.

"Something I teach beginning students in ballet."

How was she going to phrase this?

Gary had a significant slouch.

Was it a congenital defect?

A lack of self-awareness?

Or the sum of life disappointments, defeat, and despair?

"Stand straight. Shoulders back. Drop your arms.

And don't let your head get there first."

It was like being in the army again.

That time, he was being yelled at during basic introductory training. Now an amazing, beautiful ballerina girl was gently coaching him. He promptly shot up. Shoulders straight.

Head high. Impeccably straight.

Felicity smiled.

"Outstanding. Perfect ballet form. A plus!"

"Never knew I was doing that," Gary added.

"All you have to remember is… don't let your head arrive at the destination first."

"Don't let my head arrive to the destination first."

Now, standing there straight, tall, and confident.

Felicity thought, *Wow. He is so much cuter and handsome.*

Street lighting revealed both their reflections in the glass, holding hands.

They really made a beautiful couple, she thought.

They turned to look at each other.

Then kissed.

Gary's first kiss.

It was the most wondrous 6 seconds of his life.

I am in heaven. This must be what heaven feels like, Gary thought as he held her.

She could tell he had a strong body.

Felt nice muscles beneath his clothes.

It must be because he was in the army.

And she felt Gary's heart pounding as she held him against her. *His muscles are some sort of armour,* she thought, because he was so sensitive inside.

"Your heart is beating so fast."

"I'm sorry."

She touched his chest.

Cupped his face in one hand.

Kept her other hand on his chest.

"It's so nice."

What was what happening?

He didn't want this to ever end.

She held her palm against his chest feeling his racing heart. They kissed again.

His heart must be going a hundred miles an hour.

He really, really likes me, she thought.

They held each other.

He touched her face.

She's from heaven, Gary thought.

"Your skin is so soft," he said

Felicity smiled.

One hand remained on Gary's chest.

So amazing, this is so amazing, she thought.

The life in him beating away…

I love her, Gary thought as he looked at her.

It was so sweet.

He is so sweet.

He is it.

The closest thing ever to finding her Mr. Perfect, Felicity felt and thought.

Chapter 11

That was one sweet date, Felicity thought when she arrived home. All was quiet. Nanna and Daddy had retired, and an envelope was sitting on the kitchen table waiting for her.

When she read the contents, she screamed.

Juan, the illustrious discoverer of dance talent from New York, announced she had been selected to star in this winter's rendition of 'The Nutcracker' at Place Des Arts. Thence it would be Broadway. Stardom. The world.

That weekend a function was held to make it official.

The entire Montreal dance community gathered representing Jazz. Classical. Ballroom. Ballet.

Her grandmother. Daddy. Nancy.

Hanna where there. Dick too. Debonair and smiling.

Kisses. Handshakes. Claps. Cheers.

Champagne spewing all over.

Tears of joy dripped down Felicity's cheeks as her daddy hugged and kissed her.

"Your dreams are finally coming true."

While everyone was mingling,

Gary had a pop in his hand and was standing off the entire time in the corner alone.

Felicity noticed this during the evening and now was able to walk up and speak to him.

"Sorry, I couldn't chat sooner."

Crowds unnerved Gary but to see her shine made him glad. He was even more in awe of her now and the wait of being with her a few moments was worth it.

"The world has discovered how amazing you are. Thanks for letting me know you," he said.

Felicity wanted to hug and kiss right there and then.

He felt so too, but something was amiss.

"What's wrong?"

Gary pointed up at the clock.

"8:30. Have to catch the bus. 9 o'clock soon.

Scary people out there."

She was going to take the initiative and do something about that phobic issue of his as soon as she got the chance.

"Congratulations and good night," he said.

"See you soon," Felicity replied.

Hanna had observed Felicity briefly conversing with Gary whom she didn't know and was speaking to May as Dick approached from behind ready to top-up their glasses with more champagne.

"Who was that young man Felicity was speaking to?"

Dick froze, curious of May's opinion of Gary, unaware he was eavesdropping behind in the hubbub of the crowd.

"I am sure he is going to be her first official boyfriend," May happily announced.

Hanna was stunned.

"Is he a dancer?"

May smiled. "No, she told me he is her Mr. Perfect."

Dick nonchalantly stormed off without anyone noticing. Never had the blue blood boiled in Dick's veins like it did at the moment. Furious with Felicity for being so foolish.

Fuck it, he had move quick.

This was going to get ugly fast.

*****

Speeding down Sherbrooke Avenue in his Vette minutes later, on his cell phone

"Listen, I need to utilize your services..."

Passing some slow poke who pulled onto Sherbrooke suddenly, Dick swerved into another lane, leaned on his horn and yelled into his cell phone.

"Never mind the dirty details I'm paying you...

All you need to know is that he's a loser!"

A police cruiser was now behind him.

Flashing Lights on.

"Shit!"

Dick pulled over.

"Be in touch very, very soon…"

Dick clicked off.

He hit the side window button down as the burly cop waltzed over.

"You own this gas guzzler," the cop queried in French.

"Of course, I own this car!" Dick snapped in Quebecois.

"I.D. and registration?"

Dick shook his head and complied.

A few minutes later the cop returned and handed back Dick's insurance papers and license.

"Life and death emergency?" the cop asked.

Still primo pissed about Gary, Dick snapped back.

"What's it to you?"

"A three hundred dollar fine for excessive speeding is what it's going to be to you."

Dick tore the ticket out of the cop's hand.

"That all?"

He was going to teach this smart-ass.

The cop snatched the ticket back.

Scribbled more details.

"And an extra hundred buck fine for failing to signal when you changed lanes."

The cop tossed the ticket at Dick.

When he drove off smirking, Dick slammed his fist on the dash. Rage even more compounded now.

What did Felicity see in that blockhead Gary?

Pointless trying to figure it out.

But like the cliché goes, he rationalised, all is fair in love and war. Vette tires squealed and once again, Dick burned rubber and flew down Sherbrooke.

*****

The appointment was with the same psychiatrist at the same hospital she was institutionalised and met Gary at. She didn't want to be reminded of the breakdown but had no choice. Especially now. Never in her memory had so many good things happen to her all at once.

"How's life since we last met?" the psychiatrist queried.

"My career has taken off. I'm going to star in the Nutcracker at Place Des Arts this Christmas."

"What about in the romance department?"

"Best it's ever been. I've met two, great guys."

"Tell me about them?"

"One is rich, confident, successful, and handsome.

The other is cute and poor, but the sweetest guy in town."

"How does it feel seeing them both?"

"Horrendous. I'm torn in two different directions."

"Sounds like an opportunity."

"What do you suggest?" Felicity asked.

"Get to know them both and choose one."

"I don't feel leading them both on the same time is appropriate."

"Have you dated much?"

"Tons of guys but I don't sleep around. So my experience with men in actual relationships is zero."

She was quite a stunning young woman.

"It's simple: It's about heart. How do you feel?"

"I should go for Mr. Perfect," Felicity said.

"The sooner you do that, the better," he replied.

May prepared a special meal to celebrate Felicity's newfound success. Gary and Harry were the only other guests.

Ray was incensed because she had let him know last minute, precluding Dick.

Squash. Eggplants. Beans. Salad and Spinach.

There was one good thing about it though.

The aroma of veggie concoctions on the table wafted through the dining room causing Harry to squirm in his seat. To his finicky sense of smell, it was offensive and reeked, and Ray gloated. May entered with a roast resting on a turkey plate.

"I prepared this just for you."

Harry breathed a sigh of relief.

Thank God, he thought.

"No exotic spices on it. Just plain pepper and salt."

She could see the happy gleam in Harry's eyes.

"No garlic or garnishes on it?" her son Ray asked.

"Absolutely none," she coldly responded.

What a waste, Ray thought.

"I'll get the potatoes then we can start."

"Slovenian potatoes we had for Thanksgiving?"

Ray questioned.

May glanced over her shoulder on her way into the kitchen.

"Plain mashed potatoes just with butter this time."

Ray snarled. Glared at Harry. *Bastard,* he thought, how the hell did it happen so fast?

His mom and this old coot—lovebirds.

Look at him. All spiffy in his suit, bow tie, and white hair combed back nice and neat. That sneaky snake.

All his life Harry dined alone.

When ordering restaurant meals was entitled to request food to exact specifications. Now, swishing plain mashed potatoes in his mouth. It was the first time he did not experience stress dining as a guest in a private home.

No surprises. No grotesque tastes or textures offending his palate. May being mindful of his sensitivities seated opposite enjoying her salad, at ease, smiling.

"How is everything?" she asked.

Gary, experimenting with eggplant signalled thumbs up. "The roast beef?"

"Superb, dear," Harry replied.

Ray was aghast.

Where did he get the gumption to call his mom 'Dear'?

From a growing boy all the way into adulthood, he'd been in this same spot witnessing this play out with dozens of men. He hated himself for thinking the thought, but it was true.

His mom really was easy.

A hussy.

What was going on here?

There's no way Harry could be this clueless?

Ray burped.

Felicity and Gary laughed.

May glared over.

"Excuse me."

"How about some of your vegetable soup?"

"Yes, Gary should try Nanna's veggie soup," Felicity added.

Few minutes later they were slurping on May's famous soup. Unlike Harry's hypersensitive one, Gary's palate was inquiring, and he had never sampled anything like it.

"What's in it?" Gary asked.

"A to Z vegetables.

Everything but the kitchen sink," Ray added.

Gary chewed.

"Chunks of potatoes too?" Gary questioned.

"Yes, there is," May replied with a smile.

"Harry, try it," Gary added.

"Yes," Felicity concurred.

"It's contemporary. Spices from all over the world.

Very multicultural.

Nanna should market it Montreal style fusion cuisine soup," Felicity added.

Harry stared at them.

As a guest in various homes over the years he'd encountered this scenario before and it never ended well.

"So, what do you say, Harry?" Ray challenged.

Everything was perfect until now. No pressuring.

May preparing the meal mindful of his hypersensitive palate. Other varieties of food for everyone's tastes.

Everyone was staring—all eager for him to sample it.

"Sorry, not me."

"Oh, C'mon," Ray shot back.

Here we go again, Harry thought.

He did not want to upset May and had to get out.

"With all due respect, I'd rather not."

Initially, polite suggestions inexorably morph into nasty insistence so he had to bail.

"After all the trouble my mom went through preparing the boring roast beef and plain mashed potatoes just for you. How could you be so rude?"

Harry bluffed his way out this household on Thanksgiving and could not think of an original excuse to use now.

"Nothing to do with pride. Just not my style."

"Do it for my mom, or maybe you don't care how she feels?"

Felicity and Gary were growing very uncomfortably witnessing this. May was feeling for Harry, but Ray's comment was relevant.

"Sorry, May," Harry said.

"I understand and accept it as you are," May added.

"It's a disgrace! Try the soup! One spoon," Ray demanded. Harry had to taste the vegetable soup. It was urgent.

Imperative for May. He dipped his spoon to the bowl and was about to sample it, but if he had to spit the veggies out of his mouth the result would be worse.

"No."

"My mom, the gourmet chef, who loves food from the four corners of the world? Him? You want this clown to be your squeeze? You don't even breathe the same air!"

Harry realised it was too late.

"Get out. Go—before I throw you out myself."

Harry couldn't even face May and promptly left.

"Typical English, so cold," Ray concluded.

Good, he thought.

The idea of his mom and this geezer screwing disgusted him.

Harry strode to the busy Greenfield Park intersection where he hailed a cab. It would have been easier to engage in fisticuffs with Ray than do the alternative.

So happy to just be in her presence. To kiss and hold her hand granted him joy he never knew before.

How could he have been such a coward?

He should have risen to the occasion.

Tried the stinky soup.

*****

They were in May's bedroom.

Felicity hugging her upset grandma tight.

"Gary said your boyfriend has a skittish palate.

Instead of running to fine food like you, he runs away from it."

Felicity wiped tears from May's face.

"I never thought the day would come when you would be the strong one, Felicity."

"What do you expect? You're 86 years old, Nanna."

"I was at the doctor's. I'm sick. Dying, Felicity."

Felicity held May tight. For years her strong-willed grandmother refused to listen to doctors.

Although her mind was still sharp, Felicity noticed her grandmother physically slowing down this last year.

Gary was on the sofa in the living room when Felicity brought out postprandial desserts.

"What kind of sweet is that?"

"Apple cobbler a la whipping cream on top."

"I better leave. Your grandmother is upset."

"Last thing she wants is for this to be wasted."

Felicity sat down next to Gary and handed him the cobbler.

"My grandmother is dying."

Instead of indulging Gary put it down.

"This is no sweet moment."

"You're right."

Felicity was also forgoing dessert.

"First it was blood pressure and her heart.

The other day she learned cancer."

"The doctors say she has a chance to live a few years."

"That's good then."

"Yes, very good. Maybe we should eat."

Gary grabbed the cobbler and attacked it. Felicity likewise.

"Umm, whip cream's really good."

"Her own recipe from scratch."

"Your grandma should have been a chef."
"Too late now."
"Yes, sorry to hear that."
"I went to the hospital to see a doctor too."
Gary stopped eating.
"Everything's A-Okay," Felicity added.
"Why then?"
"It was the psychiatrist from the hospital.
We talked about changes and about the men in my life."
Gary froze.
"Men? Me and more guys?"
"Yes. And I've made my pick."
He was at a crossroads—frozen—stunned.
"I like you. I've chosen you. I want you, Gary."
How lovely she was and what he was hearing.
Even the way she sounds.
Her voice.
He fell into her arms.
He could hibernate in her softness forever.
She could feel his heart wildly reverberating against her breasts again.
Yes, she was right.
This was the man for her.
Still, she sensed unease "What is it?"
"Who is the other guy?"
"It doesn't matter."
"He's going to hate my guts."
"Too bad."
"What if he fights for you?"
"He's not the type."
"How do you know?"
"He has plenty of options to choose from."
"None of them as high quality as you."
"You're really sweet," she said.
"You don't know how beautiful you are."
"Do you trust me?"
"Yes," Gary answered.
She held him close and touched his face.

Gary hugged her hard.

She felt a rapid beating of his heart pounding against her. She was absolutely enchanted by this.
Whoever he is, she made the right choice.
The answer, a very obvious 'yes', and they kissed.

Chapter 12

Days later Felicity left the ballet academy following a workout and Dick drove up in his Vette with the window rolled down. He only spoke to Felicity once and tried calling her numerous times, but there was no response.

The only reason preventing Dick from stalking her sooner was a minus 15 Celsius cold snap that even intimidated long-time Montrealer's keeping them indoors.

"May I offer you a lift?"

"No, thanks," Felicity responded in French.

"You never returned my calls," Dick said.

"I told you, I'm seeing someone."

A space was vacant, and Dick parked the Vette.

Felicity kept walking. Dick jogged to her.

"There's something you should be aware of."

"What?"

"Your friend Gary. I thought he was a genuine fellow."

"He is."

"Since hiring him I learned something."

"Really?"

"He's a wolf in sheep's clothing."

"Leave me alone," she said in French.

"He's a party animal in disguise."

Felicity brushed it off.

That was utterly ridiculous.

"Swear it."

"How many people work for you," she asked.

"Dozens—and I screen everyone."

"It's not the same person."

"I'm telling you. He goes out drinking with the boys after shift. Chug-a-lugs beers. Chases women.

Gawks at strippers."

"You have the wrong person," Felicity shot back.

"Do not!"

Felicity halted and spun to face Dick face-to-face.

"Gary's innocent around girls. Doesn't smoke. Drink. And I'm sure doesn't get invited to parties."

"You've been played."

"Why are you doing this?"

"May I be frank?"

"You better be after making those slurs."

"A fine woman like you should not be subjected to this."

"You're full of crap," she said in French.

Felicity stormed off.

He grabbed and spun her around.

Instantly went from handsome and debonair to creepy.

"Take your hands off me!"

"It has to end before he disgraces you and your family."

The town house site on the West Island in Ile-Bizard was almost complete. Painters touched up. Landscapers unrolled cultivated lawns. Gary and labourers dumped the last strewn debris in bins.

A beat-up pickup drove up, engine sputtering, coming to a stop. Everyone froze when a voluptuous blonde exited the vehicle.

"Whoa." Claudio, a labourer, Gary's partner for the day, commented. He too moved to Montreal but from New Jersey and had recently married a Canadian woman.

Heather was dangerously dressed.

Shorts and a tank top left nothing to their imaginations.

Foreman clicked off his cell as she walked up.

Gary was even awestruck, admiring her.

"My ex on site," Heather asked.

"Jake's on another job," the foreman answered.

"On my way home from aerobics. Looks like I won't make it."

Heather saw sick puppy dog guys drooling and smiled back.

"Anyone able to help a girl out?"

Everyone was caught off guard by the overture except Claudio, who stepped forward.

The bigwig who hired him had paid well.

Only thing he had to do was keep his trap shut to get a 500 buck bonus coming to him if it played out.

10 minutes later, Claudio was tinkering with her engine under the hood. Heather was bent over and revealing cleavage. Construction workers and labourers stood swooned, gawking, and leering.

"Hold it right there. Clip that down."

Heather pressed her finger against the latch.

Claudio glanced at Gary in the driver's seat.

"Now."

Gary turned the key and the engine sputtered.

"Step on the gas."

Gary complied.

The engine started.

Heather cheered and hugged Claudio.

"Thanks a billion!"

Claudio glanced at that body of hers.

"Anytime. Any day."

Gary stepped out of the car.

Heather hugged Gary.

"For your help too."

Labourers and construction workers watch stunned.

Gary's faced was flush when she let go.

Her body pressed against him sent hormones raging and he was turned on.

"It was nothing," Gary replied.

"I'd like to treat you guys to say thanks."

"Love to—but the wife wouldn't go for that,"

Claudio replied.

Heather glanced at Gary.

"That's okay."

"Don't you want to be friends?"

Gary was completely caught off guard and speechless.

"You married too?"

"No," he answered.

"Gay?"
"No,"
"I won't bite… unless you give me permission."
Construction workers heard and catcalled out.
Gary looked at her.
She was curvaceous and had a sultry smile.
If he didn't know Felicity, he would have said yes.
"What's wrong?"
Again Gary stood there speechless—in shock.
"Just want to buy you a drink."
Gary just looked at her stunned.
"Pretty please," she said.
Construction workers whistled, cheered.
One yelled out.
"Jake won't like it?"
"Only if you tattle-tale."
"C'mon. You're cute."
More cheers.
The foreman grinned.
Heather opened the pickup door.
Practically shoved Gary inside.
Everyone on site howled.
Heather drove off with Gary riding inside.
On the drive over, she kept glancing over, smiling.
"You like me?"
Gary looked at her. She was very voluptuous.
Had long legs and an overflowing bosom.
I could easily have sex with her, he thought then thought about Felicity and knew that would be dead wrong.
"Better idea if you let me off at a bus stop."
"C'mon, I know you want me."
"You're very pretty, but I have a girlfriend."
They stopped at a red light.
Heather placed her palm on his thigh.
He was getting an erection, and she could tell.
"What she doesn't know won't hurt her."
Gary thought about the idea. Heather was right.
"But I'll know," he said.

That flustered her.
She glanced at the erection in his pants.
He's hot to trot.
Dick wouldn't put her up to something this underhanded if Gary was a sweetheart?
"You have a nice face. You know that?"
Gary was dumbstruck.
Why was she saying this?
He never really knew any girls growing up.
The ones he did never said things like this.
The light changed, and the car lurched on.
"Could you please drop me off on the corner?"
"Tell you what, if you still feeling bashful after a drink, I'll be a good girl and take you straight home."
Gary couldn't figure it out.
Why was she being so nice to him?
He didn't have anything.
What could she want?

*****

It was at a sports bar in Dorval.
Harry lived close by.
Harry knew he really liked Felicity.
If Harry saw them, how would he explain being here with her? Soon as they entered Gary excused himself to go to the men's room.
She asked him what he'd like to drink and Gary told her a pop. He didn't need to pee. He just needed to get away.
He couldn't reason right around her.
Those breasts and long legs.
She had such a sensuous body.
He was ashamed of himself for having this erection and wanting her.
Felicity was sexy. But super sweet, soft, and kind.
And, he loved her.
That was the difference here.
One beverage and he'd go.

Like the jets, he could hear overhead through the roof taking off above. A server delivered drinks to the table.

"Your shots and soda pop for your friend."

When the server left, Heather reached in her purse, took out a small pill, dropped it in Gary's drink, and watched it dissolve.

She jumped as Gary materialised dropping onto a seat.

"Hi."

"I ordered a cola for you."

"Thanks," Gary said.

She was still trying to figure out the 'why' in this?

"You religious or something?"

"No," Gary answered.

"Why don't you drink?"

"Because I'm on medication."

"What kind of medication?"

Gary did not want to disclose he was taking medication because doctors said he had a mental illness.

"Would you mind I not say?"

"Why?"

"It's embarrassing."

Heather grinned but thought, *Yuck.*

So that's it.

Now she knew what Dick was up to.

This Gary has the clap or gave the dose to some woman that likely gave it to Dick.

Heather handed Gary his cola on the rocks, clinking glasses with him before downing her 1st shooter.

She watched Gary sip his drink and swish ice around the glass.

"How is it?"

"Very nice, thanks," Gary replied.

At the other end of the sports bar, Felicity and Dick were seated at a table observing.

A tear ran down Felicity's cheek.

"I'm sorry, and I hate to say it, but I told you."

"What's he doing?"

"He's a player trying to score."

Felicity quietly wept.

He hated to resort to such underhandedness but good, Dick thought. His objective was to break Felicity to remake her.

Gary felt flush, hot.

The lounge was wall-to-wall mirrored. He looked over.

His vision was getting blurry but could still see reflections.

His face turning beet red.

And now getting dizzy and starting to sweat, he gulped the rest of the cola down.

Instead of cooling him off, it made him feel worse.

Gary could hardly stand. When he did, staggered.

"I feel sick. Like I'm going to faint."

Whoa, Heather thought.

The expression on Gary's face unsettled her.

Something about this guy she couldn't pinpoint and the drug Dick gave her was more potent than he claimed.

"Why is this happening to me?"

That asshole.

She was starting to suspect Dick had retained to use her for something wicked and he was the real creep in question, not Gary.

"Listen, stay put. You don't look well," she said.

Gary propped his arm across the table to support himself up.

"No, No, no. I've got to get out for air quick."

Felicity was crying now.

Dick placed his arm around her.

"I told you he was a sponge."

Dick used a tissue to wipe tears from her eyes.

"You'll be fine, Felicity."

"No, I won't. It's not right. This can't be true?"

"Doll, you just didn't know him as well as you thought."

"Gary doesn't drink," Felicity said between crying.

At the other end of the bar, Gary frantically trying to find his equilibrium.

"Why is this happening? What's going on? I'm not crazy.

I really feel super sick…"

Heather stood up. Gary took two steps and reached out.

"Help… I can't…"

Something over how clueless he seemed made her conclude there was no doubt about this now.

Dick, that bastard, was the real S.O.B, in question here.

Construction workers acquainted with Gary from the Île-Perrot townhouse site were also having beers.

Dick made some guys privy to what was going down but did not reveal the true personal motive.

"He's trying to put his face into her tits!"

It appeared like that in the distance.

In actuality, Gary fell. Heather caught him just in time.

"No!" Felicity screamed in response, observing from afar.

Heather propped Gary down against the wall.

What happened? Why was this happening?

There were no garbage men?

He didn't do anything wrong?

He wasn't shot? It didn't hurt but felt like he'd been hit.

He was at war again.

A covert one this time.

Some Sniper had taken him out with an invisible bullet.

Patrons ran over.

He looked up at blurry faces.

Heard crying.

Felicity was looking down at him.

He reached out.

With all his might wanted to be in her arms.

Tried to stand but fell.

Last thing he remembered before lights out was even her weeping was delicate and sweet.

Patrons were yelling for a doctor.

Dick had Felicity in his arms, but her crying had escalated into bawling.

"I waited so long to find him, and he was just right."

"Sometimes life is not fair."

She cried more. He held her tighter.

"I'll terminate him for what he did to you."

"Now I have to go back to being alone just like before."

"No, you won't, you'll have me."

Felicity shoved him away.

He was stunned by her lashing out.

For a second worried she knew what he had done but dismissed the thought as something only a mentally ill person, such as the way Felicity was acting right now, would assume.

"Take it easy, Felicity…"

"You have no idea!" She yelled back.

He opened his arms.

"Come here, Felicity."

How could she? Gary was gone. She felt like dying.

"What's the point!" she yelled back.

"Let me comfort you," Dick calmly responded.

"Why live!"

Dick slowly moved towards her.

"I'll never find another guy like him!"

"Yes, you will. You'll have better. You'll have me."

Dick held out his hand.

"Please, come to me, Doll?"

"Come to him?"

She was lost without Gary.

This whole thing happened after his horrible slur.

And wealthy and handsome as Dick may be, was incapable of understanding how heartbroken and devastated she felt without her Mr. Perfect.

She snatched a steak knife off a table, slashing her wrist, severing an artery. Blood sprayed all over the walls.

Patrons screamed.

Dick scrambled to stop her from harming herself more.

"Let me die! Let me die!"

Felicity yelled as Dick wrestled the steak knife from her and passed it to a burly male patron.

"Get a first aid kit! Call 911 now!"

Dick tore a strip of table cloth and wrapped it around Felicity's wrist to staunch bleeding. Horrified patrons watched helplessly, and he hugged Felicity tight while she sobbed.

Dick met eyes with Heather, glaring viciously.

That tramp better not go to the cops, he thought as she flounced out exiting, furious with him and disgusted with herself for abetting such a horrible thing.

*****

May and Ray argued on the way home from yet another visit to the doctor. Cancer detected was worse than previously diagnosed. Oncologist elaborated treatment would be difficult for a woman her age and at best prolong life for 6 months.

May decided quick. She was not going to subject herself to chemotherapy and jeopardize remaining golden days.

She despaired but would not succumb. Felt fortunate, if anything, knowing she had one last year and was going to do everything in her darn power not to squander it.

"Listen to me. Harry is important. We were childhood sweethearts," she pleaded with Ray.

Ray had always deferred to his mother's wishes.

Now that her illness was a confirmed fact, realised she needed understanding, which he felt still difficult to give.

As far as he was concerned Harry compounded the problem.

He wanted his old mom back. The matriarchal, ball busting bitch. The strong woman who moved on instead of taking crap from good-for-nothing men she ended up with.

"You have me and Felicity. We are family who know and love you most."

"Harry's coming along for the ride too."

The idea his mom indulge in a last fling infuriated him.

"How can you choose him over us?"

"Harry is no ordinary man."

"We love you—cooking—vegetable soup and all!"

"I bring joy to his life, and he returns it to me."

Ray couldn't forgive or forget his mother's past.

Dragging him around town as a little boy, never knowing who his next daddy was.

No way wanted to remember her final days like this.

"You're dying! You should be with us!"

May broke down.

"You don't understand!"

"Explain it to me!" Ray lashed out.

"He makes me feel like the innocent, young woman I once was once in love."

They arrived home to a recorded message on the phone.

The emergency mental health unit at the hospital called numerous times.

A psychiatrist informed Ray and May the news via taped message. Felicity had a 2nd nervous breakdown and attempted to kill herself again. May collapsed when she heard that. An ambulance rushed her away, sirens blaring.

The cardiologist later told Ray her heart just couldn't handle the stress. Ray was also informed of the severe plague accumulation in her arteries. The day's earlier prognosis of a more aggressive cancer and the news about her granddaughter Felicity emotionally overwhelmed May resulting in a myocardial infarction or in laymen's language, heart attack. After being sedated, Ray was informed May's condition was critical at best.

How could she be so easy mark for this? "Harry?"

A woman with her vast experience with men.

Turned into an emotional mess?

Like some naive school girl.

Had some unknown side of his mom emerged?

Or maybe she had a delicate side like his daughter Felicity?

After all those years and relationships, could this be who his mom really was? Ray sat long-faced in the waiting room hours before he met the team of psychiatrists.

They said the incident revolved around two men Felicity presume ably was romantically involved with. That her emotional reaction to circumstances caused a mental collapse. He was not even permitted access to the mental health pavilion to even hug and comfort his daughter.

If that old geezer Harry never brought that Gary guy from B.C. to Thanksgiving dinner, this would not have happened. He knew it was insane when he heard it.

No one moves from Vancouver to Montreal. A pal in the trades once told him if it's not raining, you can work outside all winter in Vancouver wearing just a sweater. Only a lunatic would go from that to endless months of freezing hell in Montreal.

Who was going to look after Felicity now? Except for a few odd jobs, she never worked much. She'd been blessed with beauty and talent to dance and now that her moment to shine was on the horizon, it was shot to hell.

Even the backup dream he planned for his daughter, to be rescued by rich prince charming Dick, was likely down the drain. Unless boozing and watching hockey with his buddies after work he never was one much for socializing.

His one and only wife passed 5 years into marriage.

Felicity and his mother were all he ever knew and had.

And he didn't even recognise his mom anymore?

Had lost her in a month to some old guy who walked around in a bow tie and suit putting crazy romantic fantasies in her head.

And his baby girl destroyed in the prime of her life because of mental illness. What a tragedy. What a horrible day.

Worst of his life. He wanted to scream. Tear his hair out.

Toss himself off the hospital roof like some mentally ill person himself to end the anguish.

Chapter 13

Harry gawked at the phone. Just couldn't call. Didn't know where to start or how to explain he wasn't a coward for not trying the stinky vegetable soup.

Years ago, a co-worker aware that he was finicky with food invited him to dinner. Meat loaf was the main course.

The company and conversation flowed well at the start. Harry detected his co-worker's wife smirking. She heeded the warning not to put any onions in the food from her husband but later, when following the recipe, learned to do so would zap the essential flavour of the dish and leave it bland.

So she came up with the solution of grinding onions to a pulp in a blender, then mixing it in to the scratch ingredients of the recipe. She shredded the onions at such a high power the blender overheated and blew a fuse. Realising she missed a last chunk of onion on the table and already incensed at having to capitulate to such a nonsensical request, threw in the last chunk of onion in the batch assuming there was little chance the one guest who was fussy would happen upon it.

Then it happened. Harry accidentally bit into a chunk of onion and on reflex spit it out of his mouth onto the dinner table to the horror of revulsed guests.

Harry's shocking action was followed by a dinner debate. Openly out Harry was notoriously finicky with food would be the theme of the entire dinner conversation after the incident. Defending Harry, his co-worker chastised his wife.

He warned her not to put onions into the main course and accused her of being a barefaced liar for saying she didn't.

The co-worker's wife argued Harry tasted it. Was eating it. Enjoying it and it was fine. That he didn't even detect the onions in it. And she was right. Harry had polished off most of the meat loaf, and it was tasty.

And that his hypersensitive palate didn't detect one iota of onion till biting into the chunk at the end.

The bottom line was it didn't change the fact it still was untrue, Harry's friend and co-worker contended.

His co-worker's wife countered asserting it was a sacrilege to waste food. People were starving to death in the 3rd world. And Harry was a brat to insist she cater to his personal preferences at the expense of the group.

"What if he was allergic to something? It could have been deadly. He could have died," her husband argued back.

The audacity of it incensed her. She went to the trouble to specifically grind the onions into powder all for Harry's sake, ruining her blender in the process.

And if he knew anything about gastronomy, the melange of basil, oregano, pepper, salt, copious tomato sauce, with pulverized onions mixed in the ground beef, resulted in a meat loaf concoction that gave it a delectable flavour, feel, and taste.

Harry sat humiliated as guests debated over who was wrong or right. His wife was more right.

He was an invited guest.

It wasn't a restaurant where he was paying for a personally prepared meal. His co-worker's wife was put in a compromising position and forced to be evasive by the one chunk of onion thrown into the batch for not wanting to waste food.

He never once described how the chunk of onion tasted. Later read onions were tasteless when cooked. Which was what he recollected and the exact case at the time.

The texture not the flavour of the cooked chunk of onion almost made him puke. Since that time, instead of relaxing to enjoy the company after that, found himself uptight, on guard, and filled with dread when he gathered with people to break bread. Got the jitters whenever invited to dinner from an already limited social circle of married, male co-workers.

The idea of the main course being seasoned, garnished, or marinated with leeks or piquant exotic spices by one of their wives unnerved him to dread.

There was no way to deal with this fatal flaw save for making excuses. From then on he was always out of town.

Visiting a sunny destination or off the radar during the dinner filled, festive season. Invitations were years in between after that.

Reflecting back, he should have just been fashionably late and only showed for dessert. The people and connections he could have made. Perhaps there was a compatible lady he could have met. They were all gone now.

He had blown it. All those empty years. Till now. Till May again. He was not going to wallow in self-pity. He had to take action and snatched the phone off the cradle. He had to make a go for it again and get May back. He was not dead yet.

At first, Harry didn't understand a word of the rant.

It was coming out fast, in loud, spewing Quebecois French. He tried to interject, but the insults continued. Although he didn't speak or socialize with the Quebecois, he recognised words from the onslaught having lived here 80 plus years.

"Stupid. Spoiled. Scheming."

Lucky Harry didn't show up at the hospital, otherwise,

Ray would have dealt with him construction worker style and punched his lights out on the spot. If that didn't work, he would have strangled the English bastard. Ray's blood was boiling after what happened to Felicity and his mom, and he was venting the hurt out on the old coot. Harry continued to listen on the line.

"I don't understand a word of your blabbering."

So, Ray now verbalized the violence in English.

"You senile, dumb, sleazy creep!"

Harry stopped. In between, he could detect Ray was crying.

"Please, Ray? Where is she? I tried calling for hours.

Again all morning. Phone keeps ringing non-stop."

"You idiot! She chose Big John over you," Ray shouted.

"Only because I didn't fight for her when I had the chance,"

Harry answered.

"You have no idea who she is! She's a party girl!

My mom and you are not made for each other!"

"Knew her before you were born. She'll always be as sweet as the day we met," Harry said.

"You're a home wrecker! You destroyed our life!"

"I love May," Harry yelled back.

"I'm wrong! You're worse. You're dumb. They don't make them any dumber. That's dangerous to all of us!"

Harry persisted, trying to try reason again.

"Please Ray, give me a chance…"

"Never!"

"It's May's life. I'm her sweetheart now!"

Ray laughed.

The tone caused a pang of dread to sweep through Harry.

"She had a heart attack!"

A year was siphoned from the physical force of his life.

The words hurt Harry as much as being physically hit.

"A heart attack! She's going to die. You hear me, Harry!"

"HOW DID THIS HAPPEN?" Harry cried out.

"Never pretended to like you or that lunkhead Gary from Vancouver!"

"What hospital? Where is she?" Harry demanded.

"You mucked up our lives," Ray added.

Even though he knew it was untrue, Ray could not resist having the last word to vent his pain.

"It's all your fault, sayonara, Harry."

"NO," Harry cried out, and Ray clicked his phone off.

Harry turned to stone. Dropped the receiver.

It shattered on garage pavement.

It can't be over between them. Can't be.

86 years old.

All those years alone.

Meeting May again now. All suddenly not lost.

So late in his life and just to begin?

Now dreaded realisation of losing her etched lines on his face. Sucked another year of vitality from life force account.

He ran into his bungalow, dropped onto the living room couch, and wept like a little boy wailing for his mommy.

His lost, misspent life.

*****

Gary awoke in the hospital. They were at him at once.

Doctors questioned if he had smoked drugs?

He told them the only drugs he takes are his medication for panic attacks. You mean 'mental illness'? They pressed.

He told them he just takes them for feelings he gets, but doctors said a blood test was done and insisted to know the truth. Demanded to know how long he'd been experimenting with street drugs for?

Gary told them he never took dope in his life.

Was even feeling better and been the happiest he had ever been since getting a girlfriend. The way they looked at each other frightened Gary after that.

Soon as they left the room, he slipped off the hospital smock. Couldn't recollect exactly what happened but knew he didn't do anything illegal yet felt like he was supposed to be some sort of criminal. The only sense Gary could make of what happened was bad. Real bad. He jumped in his jeans and jacket hanging on the chair.

Feelings similar from the time he escaped Ottawa to Montreal when doctors pronounced him 'schizophrenic'.

They didn't voice it, but the way they were whispering motivated him to skedaddle out of the hospital room quick.

*****

7 a.m. Sunday morning Heather drove her Lexus through empty Montreal streets. Bells from the Queen Mary of the World Cathedral chimed. A few die-hard churchgoers headed to Mass, and a lone jogger in a tracksuit sprinted by.

Jesus freaks and fitness freaks, she thought.

She turned up world-famous nightclub lined Crescent Street, passing now silent bars. Party animals were home hung-over or passed out now. She turned on Sherbrooke. Entered the underground parkade of the skyscraper where that prick Dick kept an office.

When she came in the arrogant S.O.B. was smirking, kicking back with his feet propped on the desk.

"You lowlife bastard."

"They'll be all right."

"Three thou as agreed. Well done."

He was hardly giving a thought to what he had done.

"Keep your dirty money!"

His smirk vanished, replaced by a glare.

"How dare you judge me? You're a stripper!"

"I'm going to the cops."

"Do it and they'll nail you for aiding and abetting."

"You're slime," she said.

"Take the dough and get out!"

Heather snatched the envelope. Threw it.

The envelope hit Dick in the chest and burst.

50 dollar bills scattered all over the office.

"Peel my clothes for desperados every day before I ever accept your dirty money."

She marched out. For a few seconds, he was worried.

He had better make some calls to cover his tracks.

Then dismissed the thought, realising he was being ridiculous.

That whore reports him she'll be in just as much shit.

*****

Gary worried police were coming to his place and arrest him for breaking out of the hospital, but they didn't show up. No doctors called either. Monday he took the Metro Bus out to West Island to go to work like nothing happened.

It was such bad manners. Instead of helping, a clique of labourers sat watching Gary load heavy shards of drywall and lumber into the bin. They were leaving him to do all the dirty work at the end while laughing and making comments in French.

He was pretty sure the message of it being of how dumb or what a joke this English guy was. When the comments shifted to English, it happened.

"Did you hear the news? For the next townhouse project, Dickey's hiring a new guy!"

"Yea, hear he's a better man than Gary!"

Their laughing frightened Gary, and he picked up debris faster, tossing it in the bin. Gary stumbled. They laughed.

"Looks like he's feeling the heat!"

Laughs. Gary noticed his hand was shaking as he picked up empty paint cans and dropped them into the bin.

"So, big date tonight again, ha Gary?"

Gary glared at them.

"No," one of them snarled mockingly.

"Hear he's got another date with that hot chick with the big titties," another said laughing, and high-fives followed.

Fear of them was morphing to anger.

Gary stopped working and glared at the slackers.

"What the fuck you staring at? Finish the job."

That was it. He didn't have to take this. Gary dropped the drywall he was holding and began to walk away.

"Did I say you can leave?"

Gary ignored the lug and continued walking.

"Hey, asshole. Freeze. Stop right now."

"No," Gary responded assertively.

He was going to walk straight to the bus stop.

Even if he had to wait half an hour for not checking the schedule.

Burly construction worker sprung to his feet.

Sprinted over, blocking Gary's pathway, causing him to stumble and stop. Others laughed.

"What the fuck you doing?"

"Why," Gary shot back.

He grabbed Gary by the lapel.

Was in his face.

"You don't ask questions, I do."

"You're not in charge."

"Did I hear that right?"

Gary looked at all of them.

They were a gang. One of them spit something out of his mouth. Some laughed.

"Now, what did you just say?"

"You're not my commanding officer."

Gary was about to step away, but the big goon seized him.

"Well, I just elected myself chief. Now, clean the rest of this shit up, and if I feel like it, I'll let you go…"

He remembered the sports bar from last Friday and the feelings he had before passing out.

It was beginning to feel like he was going to war again.

"Your turn now," Gary said.

The gang laughed. Gary tore away from the grip on his chest and began to walk away.

"Stop right there. Or I'll kick your fucking ass."

Gary kept walking. He was leaving for good.

"Did you hear what I said? Or are you deaf and dumb too."

Gary took another step. The burly labourer charged.

As he grabbed, Gary turned and using momentum, flipped him over the side of his hip, whiffing a slipstream of liquor breath and sending him to the ground. He learned to do that while training to be a paratrooper before going to Afghanistan.

Everyone looked on, stunned.

"I don't work here anymore," Gary added and walked off.

*****

Ms. Jepson received a message on her personal cell phone. Didn't recognise the number but scrolled down the list of names and saw Gary next to it. Jarry—her client who came to Montreal from Vancouver. He did not speak French nor had family here.

His message indicated he was riding the bus back from his job at the construction site on the West Island to Lionel

Groulx Metro stop and transferring to another bus before arriving at the welfare office.

She had given him her personal number and knew by the tone in his voice something went wrong. Her first reaction to what he told her was rage. She never got angry with clients but did now because he had come so far.

"Quit—*Pourquoi*? Why, Jarry?"

"They were making fun of me."

"You'll have to go back on assistance!"

"I know."

"*Ne comprends pas*—you don't understand, Jarry?"

"What?" He asked.

"*Couper l'argent*—they're cutting benefits."

"I'll eat pasta 3 times a week to save money."

"Plus de 20%."

"I'll skip meals. Buy a bus pass every 2nd month."

"You're going to be homeless, Jarry."

"No, I won't!" Gary shot back.

It was the first time he raised his voice to her and immediately regretted it.

"You won't be able to afford it, Jarry."

"I'll find a way," he fired back.

"Non vous aider. I can't help. To live there, you had to have a job…"

"I did it. I was employed."

"You stopped. They're going to evict."

"I'll go to a shelter."

"There's no room, Jarry."

"I'll find an abandoned building. Camp inside."

"The city is tearing down condemned buildings."

"I'll ride the metro bus at night."

"They stop at 3 a.m.?"

"I'll wander till five when they start again."

"With drug dealers and criminals, Jarry?"

"Doesn't matter. I'll take my chances."

"A homeless client overdosed. Another homeless client was robbed of his welfare money and murdered last week."

His social worker Ms. Jepson looked worried and upset when he left. She had believed in him. He had so much promise.

As part of the experiment to aid clients most able to extricate themselves from poverty, the provincial government paid the damage deposit and 1st month's rent for them to live in favourable living conditions to aid their plight.

Jarry had been given the time and succeeded, but his victory was short-lived. Now would be unable to afford or pay next month's rent.

She never would have entered the world of social work if she didn't care about the vulnerable. In certain instances, one became personally involved with those you were trying to help.

Now she was obligated to notify the landlord immediately.

Montreal was one of the most desirable and liveable cities in the world. Masses of people here lived functional, productive, and for the most part happy lives. They worked. Had families. Loved. She was of both worlds. Drove a nice car. Had a full mouth. House paid and comfortable place to sleep. Possessed physical and mental health. Had five weeks' vacation. Knew no privation and was financially fit to make choices she wanted.

While the normal functional world happily carried on day to day her clients the mentally ill. Crippled. Drug-addicted. Charity cases and dispossessed struggled with poverty. They smelled. Were lazy. Ignored. Looked down on. Waved off. Told to step up.

How could the happy and productive not reflect a moment and consider a person alone and despairing on the street really was not broken but an individual with no one to love them enough in the world to take the time to follow through until their pain or dysfunction was healed.

She had lost Jarry. And it had pained her to think of his rise and looming descent. It was heartbreaking, and she witnessed it on a few occasions in her career before.

Ones who almost made it. Were certain individuals in the world predestined to lose?

No, she refused to accept anyone was born to fail.

After receiving information about Jarry, the Landlord informed the owner. A development occurred, and the owner was placing the building for sale in two months.

Reliable tenants in place would make the property more appealing to potential investors, so the subsidized individual under the auspices of social services had to be out.

After catching the bus from Pie-IX metro station and disembarking Gary saw the sign displayed on his 4th floor apartment window 'A LOUER'. He didn't know many French words but knew that meant 'For Rent' and broke out in a run.

He had to speak to Felicity. The incident at the sports bar had been haunting him since he left the hospital. When nothing happened, hoped the mess would fade away like a bad dream.

It was terrifying at the time, but the feeling passed as the reality of another day began. But he had not heard from Felicity since and was growing panicked and anxious.

He left a message after message. She always called back within minutes. He waited hours and heard nothing. Called again and again. Then he was pleading. Begging her.

He wanted her.

Needed her.

If she could hug him the pain he was feeling would be healed. But she never answered the phone.

Where was she? What happened?

He missed sweet Felicity and not being able to hold her hurt.

Harry didn't answer either.

He left messages for May too.

She had given Gary the family cell phone number and also did not respond.

Gary even left messages with Felicity's father Ray.

No one called back.

No one answered.

He had lost his job.

He would soon lose his place with the nice view.

Even taking medication could sense the dungeon of doom creeping up.

Something really bad was going on.

Not what the psychiatrists described as 'irrational feeling or mental illness'.

This was for real.

Chapter 14

A large bandage where Felicity slashed herself circled her left wrist. Daddy was holding her right hand, looking at her, so sad. She had never seen him look so forlorn.

"Please, don't be so gloomy," she said.

She was unaware Ray had spoken to a team of psychiatrists, and the current prognosis was disturbing.

The chief psychiatrist entered.

Felicity recognised him as the same doctor she met during her 1st breakdown. The tall, rangy one who looked like a retired basketball player.

"Bonjour."

"Hi!" Felicity replied, in her old irrepressible manner.

The veteran psychiatrist began to evaluate her state of mind with a set of innocuous questions.

She was present. In the here and now.

Knew where she was.

Could differentiate between illusion and reality.

Came across as buoyant, positive, and responsive.

"Now that we've talked this over, that I accept and understand what I did. Nothing is no longer wrong, so I should be free to go, right?"

Ray and the elder psychiatrist exchanged a glance.

"I am not suicidal anymore. You know that, right?"

Again Ray and the elder psychiatrist exchanged glances.

"Why is that so hard for you to understand? I just couldn't bear seeing Gary with that girl in the bar."

It was encouraging she was optimistic, but he had to bring cold hard facts to the forefront. If her Pollyanna persona remained stable after learning of this setback, he estimated a promising recovery to follow.

"Felicity, you attempted to kill yourself, twice now."

"But I'm taking the medication you gave me. Am feeling 100% better."

"Unfortunately, we have to keep you for further observation."

"What!" she exclaimed, indignant.

"There's going to be fluctuations in mood."

"But I feel fine."

"Exactly, feel."

"Since when is being in a great mood a problem?"

"You may be in high spirits but your brain chemistry is volatile and needs to be stabilized. That only is going to happen with time and monitoring the dosage of the powerful medications you are being treated with."

"I have a busy life to live. I'll leave in the morning and return at night."

"Not after what happened."

"You can't do this to me."

It's starting to manifest, the psychiatrist thought.

Ray braced himself.

"Do you know anything about me? I'm set to star in the lead female role of 'The Nutcracker'!"

"I'm well aware of that."

"I've trained and prepared years for that opportunity."

"Yes, and it's very unfortunate to hear."

"This is my life!"

"We can't risk it. I'm sorry the timing is so bad."

Felicity came to an epiphany.

The answer was no and going to remain no.

She didn't even think.

Adrenalin hit, and she bolted—dashing out of the room like a shooting star through a black night sky.

He witnessed patients react in his time but was stunned by the explosiveness from someone of such delicate demeanour.

She was a beautiful young woman in the prime of her life with everything to live for. It was going to be a bad one.

My poor, baby girl, is all Ray thought as Felicity left them behind in a slipstream of wind.

"Code green! Code green," reverberated over the faculty intercom as Felicity bolted down the hall like an Olympian.

At checkpoints, orderlies were thumbing through iPhones.

Playing cards. Chatting with nurses. And froze noting the emergency page. When psychobabble and medication didn't cut it, the dirty job had to be done. No problem. The bulls on duty today were beefy, old-timers known as the 'Big guns'.

But Felicity was not just another pretty face who succumbed to mental illness. She'd been working out and exercising for years, and they were going to learn that quick. As she dashed through the hall, Orderly #1 was stunned.

Holy crap was this one fast.

He didn't even have to think just lunged—Felicity jumped, ballerina side splits in the air leaving him crashing headfirst into the wall, rendering him instantly unconscious.

Orderly #2 was jolted by #1's bone-breaking collision into a wall. Whoa, compo for that cowboy for sure. He stayed cool and nonchalant. As she raced by, he suddenly grabbed Felicity.

The palm of her arm reflexively shot out, hitting him square in the chest like a steel battering ram.

The force and power coming from a slim, young woman caught him completely off-guard sending him spinning off balance. He clipped a psychiatric nurse with a tray of medications who tripped. Red, white, and blue anti-psychotic tablets flew every direction along with two pairs of upended feet.

Felicity sprinted down the hall with a surge of adrenaline. Patients cheered as she flew by. It was obvious she was on the run, and their cheers empowered her more.

Orderly #3 stood ground waiting.

He'd been a star centre lineman in high school and no wacko was going to dummy him.

But this was no football game.

He couldn't comprehend Felicity had more more to lose. It was a Super Bowl of her life, and her thin, lithe, flexible body slammed into the bulky brick shithouse, cutting him down to the floor before bursting through checkpoint #1 triggering another alarm that reverberated louder through the facility.

Psychiatric prisoners cheered.

Felicity darted full-out past physicians and nurses stunned in awe.

What in the hell is going on, Orderly #4 thought.

The 2nd alarm was blaring.

A wacko was still at large.

And then he saw her.

Man, was she flying?

Dashing like racing for a gold. This was going to be fun.

He watched as the target approached and sprang out of a corner, seizing Felicity by the wrist.

He had big, strong, fat, hairy forearms and heard his teeth grind as he smirked.

She screamed.

This was a game for him.

As he pulled to restrain her, Felicity kneed him in the groin, and he doubled over, dropping breathless to the floor.

She was free. Burst through security checkpoint #3.

Another alarm engaged. Loud. Urgent. Grating.

"Code Blue! Code Blue!" Echoed through the halls, blue flashing lights in concert. Felicity didn't care.

If anything, it inspired her even more.

This was life and death.

A major role in 'The Nutcracker'.

*****

The gig was a boondoggle.

Most of the time they thumbed through their phones or shot the shit. Orderly #5 and #6 were a team who palled around.

In instances of serious trouble backed other tiers to ensure everything was under control.

The 'Together Brothers' worked out.

Went for beers after shift.

Hung out on days off.

Liked each other's company more than their own wives.

When either worked alone or called in sick the other surfed porn or slept on the job because time dragged on and on it was so boring. And though trained to be respectful regarding patients' rights, the duo had a reputation for kicking butt.

Resident Loonies who ever got this far were few and far between. During their 15-year partnership two a year max.

And zero. No one.

None to this day ever succeeded in making it to the open doors of freedom.

Orderly #5 caught Felicity's right wrist as she zipped by and snapped a handcuff on.

"Don't think so, darling."

Orderly #6 stepped in, seizing her left elbow and swung it to be shackled. Felicity delivered a swift high dance kick that caught Orderly #5 in the chin, sending teeth flying and his lights out instantly.

She swung the shackle attached to her wrist at Orderly #6 who ducked and tackled her. It felt like she had been hit by a transport truck.

Even in her desperate, manic mindset, literally had the wind knocked out of her. Couldn't even breathe as he grabbed and lifted her up, squeezing her in a bear hug.

Felicity kicked, swung her arms and screamed.

"Gotcha," he said with a chuckle.

Felicity was prepared to fight to the death.

Wriggled with all her might.

The bitch, he thought.

Holy crap, was she full of wiry pep.

But he was powerful.

Could still bench press 300 pounds to this day.

Felicity screamed.

Used all her might.

Willed all her energy to break loose but couldn't and he laughed. Laughed! This was her life. How could he? How dare he?

She head-butted him from behind.

His vice grip slipped.

Her handcuffed arm came free.

She incorporated ballet pirouette leverage to execute a spin. The momentum of the loose cuff dangling on her wrist caught Orderly #6 across the head, lacerating one whole side of his face. Stitches were going to be required to sew the gash, and he yelped! In seconds to get his bearings back, Felicity burst through checkpoint 3.

The security breach at this access point triggered an alarm that sounded as urgent and ominous as a fire engine racing to a 10 alarm, out of control blaze. Blood was flowing profusely across his face. There was going to be a nasty scar but worse was he and his partner were in deep shit.

How in hell was he ever going to explain getting dummied by some high strung, pretty girl?

One patient in the twenty-year history of the institution ever made it this far. Felicity was the second and could see the light of the main exit-entrance doors. She used her dance conditioning for something that had nothing to do with ballet. Setting herself free from the confines of purgatory.

The moment she burst through the glass doors into freedom and sunlight knew she was going to make it. New York on Broadway and glory as a world-class ballerina was going to be.

Orderly #7 was on a smoke break when he heard the call.

A Schizoid made it past security checkpoints.

Only other time this occurred was before the 'Together Brothers' or anyone else even worked there. What happened then was out of a 1973 chop-socky, martial arts movie.

This quiet Chinese guy named Wing Wau went bananas.

Took on every orderly in the booby hatch before escaping.

Now he worried the same thing happened.

When the description of the patient over his walkie-talkie was relayed to not be an old Asian guy who was a Kung-fu expert, but a superhot girl he was relieved.

They always teased him about being bald, pudgy, out of shape, and not able to date the Nurses. But he was qualified to use the zapper and was going to show the 'Together Brothers' brains instead of brawn ruled.

The prod flicked out. Looked like a nightstick cops used.

He waited outside the doors and just tapped her with it as she emerged. Felicity tumbled down steps onto the sidewalk like a rag doll. Doctors going on duty raced over to ensure she was all right. Something more fiendish than the brutes trying to subdue her came out of left field blindsiding her, she thought before passing out.

She was loaded like a sac of offal in a rubber room by the brutes. Bruised on her thighs and back from falling down concrete steps. Previously unblemished skin on her shoulder charred where the electronic baton shocked her.

She screamed as the orderlies restrained her.

Flushed and furious this delicate young woman they underestimated, humiliated and beat them at their own game. 1# and #2 snatched an ankle. The 'Together Brothers' each grabbed a wrist as they secured her to the gurney.

The Chief Psychiatrist had no choice.

Felicity was hysterical.

A danger to herself and others.

This was no time for a subtle intravenous option.

He approached, branding a large needle.

Felicity released a hellish scream.

They yelled at a little, bald guy who looked like a troll.

He was the one instrumental for her capture and muzzled her. They robbed her of free will. Had blood lust in their eyes.

Didn't even know her.

The world is wrong, she thought as she began to pass out seconds after the needle entered her.

So wrong.

She was not crazy.

She was not deranged.

She was devastated.

Shattered when she saw Gary in the bar with that woman. Her heart was torn to shreds.

That was why she was here.

That was the only thing wrong.

I want my Mr. Perfect, she thought as everything faded to black.

*****

Gary took the medication, but it didn't work.

At 3 a.m. his heart was racing, and he couldn't sleep. Drenched in sweat and it wasn't even hot or summer outside.

An internal alarm was going off.

Danger was present.

Couldn't voice it but knew why.

Something to do with Felicity?

What happened to her?

Where was she?

He felt it in his heart—she was in trouble.

He tried to call yet again. Must have left a 100 messages. Anonymous voice recording now said her number now not in service. It was bad manners to call at 3 a.m.

The doctors and social workers would define these feelings he was experiencing as 'mental illness', but Gary knew it was not. He was not imaging a horror movie. He could feel something? Something terrible. Felt his lifeline with Felicity was in danger. He prayed to God for help not lose her.

Tried more phone numbers.

Someone picked up. It was Ray, Felicity's father.

Before Gary could speak, Ray was screaming.

"Stop calling and stay away from my daughter!"

"Why," Gary pleaded.

"It's all your fault!"

"What are you're talking about?" Gary added.

"Go back to Vancouver where you belong!"

"But Montreal is more romantic."

"Forget her! Felicity has another lover boy!"

Ray clicked off.

Then it was true.

Wasn't paranoia or his imagination.

Something bad happened.

And Felicity having a new boyfriend was bad for him.

It was Dick.

He could tell at Thanksgiving dinner he liked Felicity too. There was no way he could compete with him.

That rich guy could give Felicity anything.

Gary rested on his mattress another hour.

Tried to figure out what went on? He was on the job.

They were making fun of him.

One guy wanted to beat him?

Why would Dick even hire him in the first place?

It didn't make sense.

Or where some people just born assholes?

At 4:45 a.m. he called again.

Instead or ringing on and on or going to voice mail someone picked up.

Felicity's grandmother, May answered.

She was mumbling at first. Slurring words. She was sick.

Told Gary to come and see her as immediately.

The word ASAP rang through his head.

Emergency Forthwith. Pronto.

Words not conjured up since he was in the Forces.

Ray was unaware his cell even rang.

Felicity's breakdown and the incident involving his mother kept him up all day and night.

Now he was in a deep slumber on a chair.

May told Gary what hospital she was at and instructed him to come and see her around 8 a.m.

*****

The delay enabled the dance troupe to stretch, warm up, mingle and get better acquainted. Felicity was completely missing in action. Ray disclosed a few details to Nancy but made her swear secrecy? Juan was frantic. Felicity was two hours late. Completely unaccounted for. Acting the like some prima donna and wasn't even a star.

How dare she do this to him?

Hanna tried to appease him. Felicity trained years.

Dreamed for a chance like this her whole life.

No way would ever squander a break like this unless a matter of significant importance imposed itself.

Ray got a hold of Hanna when he arrived home from the hospital. She could tell by the tone in his voice over the phone something awful transpired before he began.

Felicity had attempted suicide again.

Was confined to a mental health facility.

Had attempted to escape and now confined indefinitely.

It was as if she was assaulted with a hammer.

All the training. Years of life and work Felicity put into it.

Years of tutelage and training—destroyed.

She witnessed Felicity bloom from a little sweetheart to a beautiful, magnificent, and accomplished virtuoso.

Felicity must be in anguish.

We're ruined, Hanna thought.

Catastrophic for both of them.

And a devastating blow to the dance company's international reputation she spent years cultivating. She had come a long way since the 1976 Olympics when she defected from Russia to remain in Montreal. There was little chance they would ever recover from this. It pained to think that at her age, she would never have the time to once again nurture and discover another natural like Felicity.

Juan learned of the news and yelled in his iPhone demanding the best replacements. New York immediately began to recall promising candidates and make arrangements for them to fly back to audition. Hanna broke the news to the troupe.

She had to remain composed, stone-faced, and steady, despite the loss, the show must go on.

"Felicity is in the hospital and I'm afraid has had to withdraw the lead role in the production."

Gasps echoed across the stage.

Felicity was one of the most promising dancers in the country?

It was a dream come true.

She was headed for Broadway.

How could this be happening?

It was incomprehensible?

*****

By 5 a.m. Gary shaved, showered, and was out.

He looked back and up at his place. 'A LOUR' for rent sign in French still in the 4th floor window.

The nice view of the Montreal skyline.

It ached knowing he would lose it.

There was a chill in the air now.

Colder than any air he ever breathed living in Vancouver.

Still, he could live here if he had Felicity to hug and keep him warm. If he lost her and didn't get another job, it was unlikely he'd have the strength to pick himself up and survive to begin in another place again.

He obtained bus directions to Notre Dame Hospital via free Wi-Fi at a coffee shop a block from his place. When he arrived, May's bed was propped, and she was finishing breakfast. She told Gary she had a heart attack but was a survivor and no way was she going to let this beat her.

She had a reason to live, and his name was Harry.

"He's going to love to hear that," Gary said.

"He never called. I haven't heard from him. You have any idea why?"

"You try calling him?"

"It won't go through."

"Something must be wrong with your phone," Gary said.

Ray had gone home to get a decent sleep.

In his haste left the cell behind.

May handed Gary the phone.

He fiddled and dialled Harry's number.

"I think the number is blocked."

"Is that possible?"

"My phone is cheap, but you can do lots of things on these expensive ones."

"He hardly knows how to use it himself," May said.

"I tried calling a hundred times too. There was no answer."

"The sneak! I bet the computer expert where he bought the phone did it for him," May added.

May told Gary it was plugged in, recharging a few hours and when it rang she answered it.

"The block must be reset after recharging," Gary said.

"Lucky for us."

May smiled.

Gary remained glum.

"What's wrong? You don't look happy?"

"I'm not good," Gary said.

"Then go to the supermarket and buy a bag of candy. You'll feel fine after you eat them up."

He was still not smiling.

She could see frown lines on his face she never noticed before.

"Ray told me Felicity doesn't want to see me anymore and she has a new boyfriend."

"You're going to have to brace yourself for something?"

Gary froze.

"Felicity tried to kill herself again."

Gary let out a whimper.

He lost her. It physically hurt to hear.

Like being shot point-blank.

Gary threw his hands on his face.

He knew it was bad.

Please, no God, he thought.

"Gary, listen to me."

He wanted to die.

He's not going to survive now for sure.

Something horrible inside seized him—doom. *I am doomed*, he thought.

"Gary, listen to me. Felicity is okay. You hear? Okay."

She was losing Gary. His expression terrified her.

Boyish countenance turned moribund ghost.

"I was there," he said.

"Gary? Gary?"

May was shaking him now.

"What happened? I want to hear your version?"

But he wanted to forget it.

His life went downhill since the incident in the sports bar.

May shook him again.

"Talk to me!"

"I-I, was at work. A girl's car broke down. We helped her start it, so she wanted to buy me a pop and say thanks.

I didn't want to, but it was bad manners to say no.

I had a cola on the rocks and passed out."

"Felicity was there with Dick?" May asked.

"They saw everything. I woke up in the hospital. They said I used drugs. I took off. When no police came looking I thought everything was safe."

"Something fishy is going on, and fish is one of my favorite dishes, so I don't take it kindly when it's wasted, spoiled, used or abused," May added.

"You don't understand. They were being mean to me."

"Who?" May asked.

"Guys on the job. So I quit. I'm going to lose my place. I'll be homeless in a week."

May hugged Gary hard.

In years of relationships.

All the crass, crude, and rotten ones she'd known.

Then Harry and Gary's sudden appearance in the sunset of her life. At first, she suspected an act but now maybe not?

She'd known smooth ones too in her day too.

Never had she encountered a species of gentle men like this. She could hear Gary quietly weeping and looked at the trail of a single tear running down his cheek.

"What do Montrealers do when it rains in life," Gary asked.

"We don't get upset. We just wait around for the sun to shine on us again."

He really is an innocent like her granddaughter Felicity.

Gary looked at her with those big, baby blue eyes.

He sure was handsome and could understand how Felicity could fall for him.

*****

From the hospital, he took the bus to the Canada Manpower Center. It was closed. He read on the doors it opened at 9:30 so he had a half hour to kill. Wind was whipping like mad as he waited and he almost left. Lucky he didn't. He was the first one in the office when they opened and marched to new jobs posted where he couldn't believe it.

Janitorial personnel wanted.

The bilingual ad read French nor English required.

You had to be responsible.

Work well alone.

Be fingerprinted and bonded to ensure you had no criminal record. A monthly blood test was mandatory to ensure employees remained clean from drugs. It was perfect for him.

You had to register at the desk because they were only going to interview 20 applicants on a first come, first serve basis. The clerk gave him the address where interviews took place.

It was a warehouse in the northeast end of Montreal.

He would go to a fast food hamburger restaurant where there was free Wi-Fi for map information then spend the rest of the day using his military training to reconnoitre the area by subway and bus. Tomorrow he would be prepared and ready.

Chapter 15

When Dick and Ray pulled into the parking lot, nurses were enjoying lunch because of the sunshine and balmy 20-degree increase in temperature. The Ferrari was obscenely expensive and wasn't one of the psychiatrists'.

One of them mentioned the elder man was the father of the dancer who almost escaped. The driver, the one they all had their eyes on, a suave hunk accompanying him, was a mystery.

Dick never visited a mental hospital before and strode through with Ray. They had been given guest badges by the security personnel glaring malevolently at them.

The guards knew they were here to see Felicity the witch who dummied them with stitches, shiners, and missing teeth.

The place certainly wasn't customer friendly.

Patients wandering around were wrecks.

Looked like zombies. The walking dead.

The realisation this place was a dumping ground for lost souls society couldn't hide in jail because they didn't break the law sent a chill through Dick.

That idiot Gary should be confined here, not the woman who could potentially be his unsullied, trophy wife. He heard horrible things about insane asylums. These people weren't possessed by devils. The Gods abandoned them.

No way Felicity belonged in this storing facility for the dispossessed. Why did she have to love that bozo instead of him? Hot women threw themselves at him constantly.

He was better. Smarter. Inordinately more successful.

Never in a million years could he imagine disadvantages to having his shit together.

What did she see in that destitute loser?

No way he could let this one get away.

It could be years before he met another one like her who didn't give a damn about his money like Felicity.

Felicity was locked in an isolated unit. So broken she couldn't even speak. She just bawled in Ray's arms. Endlessly sobbing away. On the job Ray was reliable. Had a reputation for getting the job done. But this was no being in charge of a rough and tumble construction crew. For the first time in his life, he was helpless. Powerless to save and shelter his baby girl.

Ray told the Chief Psychiatrist he brought along a person whom he really respected. At first, Dick listened detached.

But the notion of insinuating Felicity insane and disempowering her like this sickened him.

It was psychobabble bullshit.

If you fell on your ass, you picked yourself up and jumped back on the horse.

People weren't disposable weaklings you write off for life.

"Can't you see she's not one of them?"

"You qualified to make that assessment?"

"I'm someone who gives a damn."

"And I'm responsible for Felicity's well-being."

"Felicity is a professional. She's good at what she does and should be paid damn well for doing it."

"The staff has been in contact with the producer of the show, so we're all on the same page about this."

"Her time is now. You scallywags pulled the plug!"

"Shall I rephrase? We have the producer's consent."

"Let her out, or I'll sic the best attorneys to sue your ass pronto," Dick asseverated.

"You don't have all the facts, sir."

"Brace yourself for war," Dick said.

He and Ray left.

The return trip was a nerve-wracking experience for Ray.

Dick raced down Autoroute Ville Marie.

Souped up engine roaring, swerving in and out of lanes without signalling. Drivers screaming Quebecois obscenities. Flashing middle fingers. Horns blaring.

Dick not flinching an iota.

"We lost," Ray said.

A car slammed on its brakes. Dick swerved to avoid it.

"I can still get her released."

"How? Show is next week?"

"Take them to court. Get an injunction."

"Everyone will know. Might make things worse."

"Correct—and we don't have time."

"It's over then."

"You trust me?" Dick asked.

If any man was able to look after his baby girl once he was dead and gone, it was his new boss, Dick.

"Oui—yes."

"Make sure I'm cleared to see her in few days."

"I don't want to give Felicity false hope."

"Ray, listen to me. It's the last chance we have."

Dick flew to New York City first class and arrived at La Guardia airport by late afternoon.

What a colossal fuck up.

He just wanted to scare the dumb-ass off.

Instead, it destroyed Felicity.

What's done was done.

He was powerless to reverse it.

He had to take action. Clean this mess up quick.

By 7 he was in the financial district.

On the 50th floor of the Garelli Brothers Headquarters, he met one of the icon's themselves. Luckily it was Jackson, the more patient and amenable of the twins.

"Everything under control up there in Montreal?"

"It is, sir."

"What is so damn important?"

There was a chance Jackson would shit can him for being this brazen, but he'd land on his feet. He had to risk it.

"Personal matter, sir."

Dick couldn't read if Jackson was surprised or shocked.

"Involving the business?"

"To a degree, indirectly, sir."

On the flight, he considered the sugar-coated version.

He would recount minus his self-serving intention and the details of the dreadful result.

He told Jackson a young woman he cared about immensely had a sudden nervous breakdown.

A darling in Montreal's ballet community.

One of the most promising dancers in Canada.

A woman unimpressed with the finer things in life he had to offer. Described Felicity as the kind of quality female you only meet years in between. That her future was in jeopardy.

That the company's influence could ensure a positive result.

Be her saving grace.

Jackson Garelli was surprised.

Dick was a hustler.

A brash, go-getter who came across poker-faced or tenacious as a gator with teeth locked on its prey.

Dick's stubbornness secured them some damn fine properties they flipped to make serious dough on. The notion to intervene in his personal affairs was unwise. Yet for him to fly in, drop his guard, and disclose such a personal issue was a desperate measure If this dancer was worth fighting for.

A keeper for life. The woman of his dreams.

It was also beneficial for the company. Accomplishments notwithstanding, Jackson felt Dick needed reigning in.

The stability of marriage, a wife, children were consistent with the company's values or as the French would presumably say up there in Montreal, "Raison de' entre."

"My wife's in charge of the corporation's endowments to the arts; I'll run the idea by her. We'll see how she feels," Jackson said.

"I'd be enormously grateful. Thank you very much, sir," Dick said, smiling and firmly shaking the Icon's hand.

At dinner, Jackson Garelli broached the subject with his wife, June. The story her husband recounted captured her attention. After making a few calls, she grew increasingly intrigued.

It was no exaggeration.

The woman was a local dance darling and rising star from Montreal. A protégé of Hanna Burnbaum, the Russian Gymnast who had defected to Canada during the 1976 Winter Olympics. She had trained under Hanna for decades.

Now the promising young dancer's life had been ruined by a mental breakdown, and she was going to lose it all in a matter of days. She picked up the phone right away.

Her intervention was required at once.

*****

It was a good sign. An easy bus and short Metro subway ride from his place to where interviews were being held.

After reconnoitring the route on free Wi-Fi at a coffee shop, it occurred to him he was riding a Jarry bus on Jarry Boulevard, his own personal mispronounced Quebecois given namesake.

Gary stepped off at the corner and glanced up at the white street sign with black lettering. 'St. Zotique'.

Imagine that, a city street commemorating a saint whose name started with the letter Z.

That was going to be easy to remember orienting himself around town down the road if he stayed and was able to continue living in Montreal.

He could see the queue leading from the compact building as he approached. Many of them bedfellows. Down and out. Likely in the same boat as him. The only difference was Gary's appearance. He was sporting his fine and only suit and carrying a briefcase. He looked spiffy and slick. A stranger might assume he was a banker. If Texas, a sharp and confident oil executive.

Gary didn't possess the inner self-confidence but if 'the clothes make the man', he needed every outer advantage he could get. In case of unexpected anxiety during the job interview, Gary extracted his daily dosage of medication from his trademark little white envelope and tossed them in his mouth.

The gentleman doing the hiring introduced himself as 'Bill'. He looked like a football player, but when he spoke his reedy voice was more high and friendly than tough.

"Expanding cause I got a contract to clean-out half the skyscrapers in downtown Montreal."

Bill scanned Gary's resume.

"As you saw outside, I have got lots of choices.

Most of them got janitorial experience to boost them up."

"Nice, but if you give me a chance, I know I could do this job well."

Gary extracted his iPhone. Hit a few buttons.

An image of his bachelor apartment flashed up.

"Wow, very shiny."

"Thank you."

"Don't see any experience on your resume, but you sure keep this place ship-shape?"

"I was in the army. Living quarters had to be spotless or else we'd get hell."

Bill looked at Gary's resume.

He was from English Canada.

"You speak French?"

"Ad said you didn't have to," Gary replied.

No wonder no one wants him, Bill thought.

"The only thing I could do is give you a low job on the totem pole, junior janitor in training guy."

Gary hear that right? Things going so good for him today.

"Well?"

"Wonderful. I don't mind starting at the bottom."

"It's a union job. Starting pay is 14.98."

"Wow, that sounds excellent," Gary added.

"One catch…"Gary couldn't imagine what.

No way this young guy will go for it. He can do better, Bill thought, before telling Gary.

"Junior janitors work Friday, Saturday, and Sunday nights."

"I'm available immediately," Gary added.

Some young guy who didn't resist working Saturday night?

Bill was stunned.

"You understand what I said? No weekends off?"

"Yes," Gary said smiling.

Except for the Sweetest Days at month's end when he had welfare money left to buy a sweet, every day was the same for him.

Weekend commitment scared party animals, ones with piss poor work ethics and 99% of everyone else off.

Gary was in a league of his own.

"Shift runs from 7 at night until 3 a.m."

Gary gasped.

Everything was perfect till Bill said that.

"Don't you have any day shifts?"

"Janitorial engineering is done when office workers go home at night to sleep."

The transformation was ghoulish. Bill almost stepped back.

"Forgot to tell you, can't work after 9 o'clock at night," Gary said.

"Why the hell not? Against your religion?"

Everything. The whole thing was ruined.

He would have to leave Montreal and Felicity now for sure.

"Personal reasons," is all Gary could say.

Bill didn't want to lose a guy who'd work weekends.

He looked at the resume. Army 3 years. Bunch of dead-end minimum wage jobs. Instability. Travelling around a lot.

"Where you stationed when with the Forces?"

"Afghanistan," Gary answered.

"My baby brother was in country too," Bill exclaimed.

"What unit?" Gary asked.

Bill hesitated. Gary knew right away. His brother was dead.

"Killed a week before coming home."

Gary grabbed his brief case and stood up.

"Job is open if you want it."

Gary looked at Bill.

"I can't work after 9 o' clock at night."

"Call. Leave a message if you change your mind."

"Thanks for the chance," Gary said and left.

As he disembarked the bus and transferred to the green Metro line towards Pie-X station, Gary was haunted by the offer. What if he was blowing an opportunity? Maybe he should say yes? Try? The pondering grew more profound.

Staying out after nine at night would be like going back to battle. Head first straight into war. On the upside, he could keep his cosy bachelor apartment with the nice view.

He would encounter scary people. Maybe garbage men too?

From Pie-X Metro station he caught the bus which was a five-minute ride to his apartment. The trip from Jarry and St. Zotique where the interview took place 15 minutes.

As he walked towards his bachelor apartment looked up at the 'For Rent' sign in French in the window again.

If he could do it his whole life would be transformed.

He would never have to move on again.

14.98 an hour to start?

He wouldn't have to beg for public assistance anymore. Could go on a vacation to a warm place.

Have money for the Sweetest Day every week.

Staying out after 9 at night?

Bad memories would haunt him.

This was his chance.

If he won, he would be able to remain in Montreal.

Maybe get to see Felicity again.

He had to do it.

It would be the last war he would have to fight in. If failed it, at least he would die trying.

Chapter 16

Dick was back in La Belle Province at midnight.
By 9 a.m. next morning he received a call from Jackson Garelli's wife June with her complete blessing to proceed.
Dick zoomed to Place Des Arts in his Vette.
An orchestrated rehearsal was in progress starring the new lead dancer flown in from Calgary. Dick watched and waited.
During the interlude, he approached Juan and identified himself as Felicity's boyfriend. Ordered him to inform the company a misunderstanding occurred and the star ballerina was returning. Juan laughed in his face. Dick retorted with an earful, poking Juan in the chest with warnings from holy hell before leaving.
Juan gave his assistant the day off.
At the conclusion of the rehearsal learned numerous attempts from New York to contact him failed. The Garelli Brothers' endowment to the arts intervened on behalf of Felicity. Dick's ultimatum was true.

*****

Felicity was in the open with patients and recognised many from the first time when she attempted self-destruction. Bedraggled with no makeup, many male patients still ogled her.
A clique of cronies Chronics who she remembered knew Gary waved. First time here Gary inspired hope disclosing he visited a few times and was preparing to catch the next bus that went by on the street outside.
Since trying to escape her spirit was calm, but she felt worse in a new way. They pumped her with so much

medication; it made her numb. Was it better to be desperate to escape or have this dead, lifeless void feeling of nothing inside?

She dreaded never feeling excited about life again.

After what happened, losing it all. The dream she worked her whole life to make a reality and become a ballet star.

Her newfound Mr. Perfect Gary by her side. She must have been hexed by spiteful karma for wanting it all?

Ray was beaming. Dick carried flowers. The banged-up 'Together brothers' issued passes and buzzed them through. Since when did visitors enter happy visiting wacko relatives jailed in the booby hatch? Something was up, and it nagged them. They radioed confidants to be ready.

The Banshee who bruised them was roaming the halls in general population, so something was up. Ray saw Felicity staring out a window. She turned to look and darted into his waiting arms to be hugged.

"My poor baby."

"So sorry, Daddy."

"Would have done the same thing if it was me."

He cupped his daughter's face and kissed her forehead.

She looked at Dick. He was smiling grandly.

"Hi," Dick said.

"Hi," Felicity answered.

He was great looking, but she wasn't thrilled to see him after what happened in the lounge that led her to this hole.

"What's going on, Daddy?"

"I've got great news," Dick announced.

Doubtful, after what happened, she thought.

"That's nice," Felicity replied phlegmatically.

Dick handed her the flowers.

"Thanks."

She whiffed the nosegay to acknowledge his thoughtfulness but didn't feel it an appropriate occasion.

"Really. I'm serious. I mean it. Truly great news," Dick said. Her daddy was even grinning.

"What could be great news after the hell I've been through?"

"I pulled a few strings," Dick added.
"What do you mean?"
"He's got friends in high places," her daddy said.
"I don't understand," Felicity added.
"They threatened to shut down the show," her daddy said.
Felicity's heart pounded. The ambivalence terrified her.
Losing it all and winning it back was too good to be true.
"No? Impossible? Can't be," she said, incredulous.
"It's true," her daddy added with a smile.
"You're being released tomorrow," Dick added.
Felicity screamed. The whole psych ward looked over.
Two bulls were about to spring into action but froze when they saw Felicity's magnificent white smile.
"Welcome back to the show," Dick said.
Felicity hugged Dick hard and kissed him.
"The trouble you must have had!"
"The least for dragging you into it, to begin with."
"Thank you. Thank you. Thank you a million times over."
She kissed Dick on repeatedly on the cheek, giggling.
I really pulled this off.
I hit this curveball out of the fucking park, Dick thought as he looked into her gorgeous face—even without any makeup.

*****

When Felicity materialized for rehearsals like nothing happened the entire cast was floored. She simply smiled and paraphrasing Mark Twain said, "Yes, reports of my death were completely exaggerated."

*****

Juan worked the troupe vigorously.
After that debacle with Felicity, his ego was compromised and ensured every dancer felt their muscles taxed to the limit.

Every bone in their bodies from their skull, spine, to their ankles, ached getting it flawless. Ten rigorous hours for five days straight to make it 110% right.

"See you up there in Montreal," Jackson Garelli told Dick over the phone.

He and June were jetting up for a winter weekend to be in attendance opening night, and his wife personally looked forward to Dick introducing them to Felicity.

Friends, family, fans, and spectators from all over North America convened upon Place Des Arts watching entranced as Felicity and the Nutcracker Prince moved in sync to the mellifluous music of the Montreal Symphony Orchestra.

Powered by newly sprouted wings, Felicity floated through the air like an ethereal angel. Mental illness was not physical and couldn't eclipse years of disciplined conditioning.

What he did to drive a rift between Gary and Felicity was wrong, but he had succeeded and almost ruined her life in the process. But a little schmoozing inspired Garelli's wife June to intercede and save the day.

Applause, cheers, and whistles reverberated through the auditorium as Felicity took a bow. She was a bona fide star. After all the gold diggers how fortunate to find a woman of such substance. Bravo to you, dear. That is how it's done.

You get knocked on your ass and jump right back on the horse to ride another day to victory. Latent mental health issue or not, this was an attribute he wanted in a woman.

After the dancing phase passed, she was going to be a trophy wife and produce his children.

He had taken her to Sherbrooke Street the prior day and purchased an evening dress she now was wearing and looked stunning.

When introduced to Montreal's social elite held her own and charmed them all. Jackson and June Garelli were captivated by her effortless grace, beauty, and resilience.

The only question mark in the equation now was Gary who could scuttle his masterpiece. Luckily, he was absent from witnessing her triumph.

Here was a woman worth fighting for.

If Gary saw her now, he'd have a war on his hands.

Go postal or ballistic.

Use his military training and slaughter him.

But he dismissed the idea. Gary may have been capable but would never take such action. The guy was a push-over. Would follow his directionless, dead-end path.

This was Montreal.

He was isolated.

Destitute.

Unable to communicate in French.

He didn't have any options but to move on.

Likely into a wall and never return.

When Dick led Felicity out Place Des Arts, a valet opened the passenger door for her to enter his candy apple Lamborghini.

"This actually your car?"

"Third vehicle. Take it out only on special occasions."

Dick slipped on black racing gloves, and his foot hit the accelerator. The Lamborghini took off.

G-force threw Felicity's back, and she giggled.

"None of this taking the bus around nonsense like your friend Gary," he added.

First, it was exhilarating. Engine roaring like a race car.

Fast turns around downtown corner streets.

"So, how are you?"

"Excellent," she said smiling.

"Sure you feeling okay now?"

"A little overwhelmed by the excitement but, yes."

"No more anxiety?"

"None."

"Blues gone?"

"Let's leave it all behind."

"Just want it perfect," he said.

It was nice at first.

Speeding like an airplane going to take off.

She didn't want to overreact.

A perfect evening but the velocity and roar of the engine was now upsetting her.

Zipping around corners giving her the shakes.

He won't keep it up. He'll slow down, she told herself.

She braced her palm against the roof interior.

"Relax, Felicity. I know what I'm doing."

Instead drove faster.

Sensed yet disregarded her unease.

"What is it?"

Before voicing her feelings changed gears and booted it again—VROOM! Charging down the freeway.

"Talk to me, Felicity?"

"Where are we going?"

"To my penthouse apartment."

"Why so fast?"

"To celebrate your success with an exclamation mark!"

Vehicles honked as he passed, zigzagging between them.

"Could you please slow down?"

"You have to appreciate this high-performance vehicle. Sit back, relax, and enjoy the ride."

How could he be so insensitive?

She never accompanied him in a vehicle, and it was emerging as a side of him she didn't like.

"I mean it!"

Empty stretch of road—he floored it—going faster.

"Please," Felicity pleaded.

If this was a condition to dating him it was a deal breaker.

Dick kept going. Driving faster.

"Stop it!"

He smiled and shook his head.

Should she persist?

Was it ungrateful, especially after all he had done for her?

"Why?" he asked.

She thought he was a gentleman.

"I'd rather arrive five minutes late and alive than 5 minutes early and dead."

"The vehicle is not designed for Sunday driving."

He flew past and in and out between more cars.

How could he be so inconsiderate to how she was feeling?
"You cut in front of that minivan with inches to spare!"

Dick swerved to the right.

"Calm down," Dick quietly added.

"You didn't signal!"

"So what!"

"A family was in that minivan," Felicity screamed.

"I can't believe you're upset. Half the people in the world don't signal when they change lanes."

"Well, it's a personal sore spot for me, and I do," Felicity shot back.

"Give me one reason why when the idiot behind is fifty feet away?"

"It's nerve-wracking when people switch lanes! Some of us require advanced warning!"

Dick laughed.

He isn't handsome anymore, she thought.

"Let me tell you something: In my world, time is money and money is time!"

Felicity began to shed tears.

"Oh please…"

He liked women feminine but not pathetic, weak, and needy.

"Felicity, you're going to have to overcome this totally irrational fear."

He's not as kind as she thought either and it hurt.

He handed her some tissue, and she wiped her tears.

"Felicity, be strong. Please be strong."

"I am strong," she shot back.

"You well? You sure you're well?"

"Positive!"

"Then what a great opportunity to get over this phobia now!"

The nerve of him, she thought.

"I've had enough!"

"You can't be serious?"

"Let me out!"

She tried to open the passenger door.

Dick activated the child lock mechanism pre-empting it from releasing.

"Let me out!"

This was either going to make them or break them.

"I'm only doing this because I care about us."

Gripping the manual transmission stick with skill and dexterity, shifted, and floored the accelerator.

"Stop it!" Felicity screamed and broke down.

Dick smashed his fist on the dash.

"Damn it! You can't ruin this whole evening because I don't signal when I turn!"

"I thought you were a nice man?"

"I'm trying to empower you!"

The whole freeway turned brake light blood red.

Every single vehicle in every lane skidding stop.

Some spinning in circles.

When Dick turned to look back at the road, hitting the brakes was futile.

Felicity braced herself for death.

No time for regrets now.

She would be with her mother soon.

The most triumphant day of her life was to be her last.

Dick swerved once. Twice. Three times, braking hard, wearing down tire treads skidding and smoking away…

Avoided colliding into vehicles in front.

When he came to a secure stop was in shock.

"Let me out!" Felicity practically ripping the door handle off. "Now—this second," she insisted. "It's over."

Dick stared at her silently.

"You hear me!"

Was he wrong? Was she just another bimbo? No, it's just the circumstances of the moment.

"My rally driving skills saved us."

"What?"

"Skill. Did you just see the skill I demonstrated here?"

Pathetic! He was so full of himself.

How were they ever going to be a couple?

"My mother and I were in an accident years ago!"

"What does that have to do with anything," Dick shot back.

"She was killed," Felicity screamed.

"That has nothing to do with us."

"The driver didn't signal when he changed lanes!"

Showboating and pressuring—he had gone too far.

Felicity clicked the passenger door unlocked and exited.

Driver's window rolled down. Dick stuck his head out.

"You should have told me," he yelled.

She stopped to turn and face him.

"My Mr. Perfect never would have subjected me to this."

He had blown it.

She was right.

He had everything but lacked the sensitivity to nurture a relationship with her.

A damn shame and his own fault.

It was the last time he ever spoke to her.

Chapter 17

Since calling Bill and telling him 'Yes, he would do it,' Gary couldn't sleep 2 nights. He wanted to contact his social worker to tell her he needed more powerful medication so he could sleep but didn't disappointing her already by cowardly quitting his job when construction workers teased him.

Maybe he should have fought them.

He could have beaten a few but the rest would have put him in the hospital or worse he would have ended in jail.

No, now was the time to prove something more important.

Go to war again to see what happens?

He was here.

In the downtown office building on the new job working.

It was hard to understand the Quebecois guy's English because of his accent but luckily duties were straightforward.

Claude showed Gary the ropes.

Janitorial facilities.

Brooms. Mops, and shammy rags.

Disinfectants and cleansing concoctions used to make surfaces shiny from salt stained winter boots since snow was forecasted for Montreal soon.

Lastly, he was shown the garbage bins in the parkade at rear egress of the tower. Veteran cleaner Claude never saw anyone so spooked. Laughed when the terror on the baby-faced junior janitor cleaning guy that didn't speak French looked like he was going to shit his pants around the garbage bins.

He was sure Jarry was no ex-heroin addict or a jailbird so he must be one of the looney types. They were the only ones desperate enough to work Friday, Saturday, and Sunday nights. His boss, Billy, sometimes hired crazy people he felt sorry for, but they never lasted. But Bill believed this Jarry from English Canada was reliable for some reason.

Not that he didn't trust Jarry but what was up here?

Why was he so spooked?   Fuck it.

He handed Jarry the keys to the kingdom and left.

It was the weekend in Montreal.

Big drunk. "Joie De Vivre."

Enjoy your life and party.

The shift was from 7 p.m. to 3 a.m.

He hadn't slept two nights because of anticipatory stress, so was eyeing the clock on every floor when elevator doors opened, willing himself to endure.

The fatigue turned into a drilling, blaring headache.

He felt this sensation before.

In Afghanistan on search and destroy missions.

After fire fights and not sleeping for one or two days when his unit was on the run. Lucky for that.

No way the weariness was going to beat him now.

First, two hours went perfect.

Tools to his new janitorial trade fastened to the cart he pushed along. He dipped the moth in the bucket of concentrated Mr. Clean and swished back and forth, polishing the white marble floors from the 2nd to the 12th floor smooth, quick, spiffy, and as shiny as the hardwood floor of his 4th floor bachelor pad with the excellent view.

Completing the 12th floor, he watched the digital clock turn to 9:01 p.m. His heart skipped a beat. His breathing tensed. He coughed. It was if something had suddenly seized and grabbed him. He started to retch. Gag. It felt like a rope around his neck, choking him or was his own fear harming him?

When he disclosed this a psychiatrist once treating him explained success sometimes manifested into the death instinct for people against themselves.

When Gary told him 'bull' the doctor suggested it was unfulfilled sexual yearnings from the subconscious. Then he thought the psychiatrist was crazy. He hadn't even been in a sexual relationship before. And never would he have fired back at the enemy in the war if he wanted to kill himself.

The choking experiences were deadly.

Terrifying and triggered when he saw scary people or garbage men after 9 o'clock at night.

He dropped the broom. It bounced. Knocked the bucket over. A dirty trail of water flowed down the white marble floor like a polluted river. Gagging he bolted into the men's washroom. Threw water on his face. The abrupt ice water shifted some sort of signal in his brain, and the choking sensation stopped.

He looked at himself. That was weird? It was tense but short-lived. His eyes were bulging out of his head. Why would he want to sabotage himself? By the time he went back out into the hall to re-wipe the 12th floor, it was 10:30 p.m.

The anxiousness grew as he ascended the office tower floors. 13 high energy but on edge.

14 getting more spooked and anxious.

15 huge stains of sweat soaked right through his work uniform under his armpits.

16 heart palpitations.

17 sweating like a pig.

Gary exited the elevator on the 18th floor.

Stopped to look at his reflection in a mirror.

The choking did not return.

Now he was drenched in sweat right through his uniform.

So overwhelmed by fearful fantasies, it was like he was lugging an 80-pound rucksack when he was in the army in a 100-degree heat dessert.

After he completed mopping the 18th floor, he ran into the men's washroom, tore off his shirt, and splashed cold water over his face and chest. It cooled him off then his heart began racing again. Then the choking and he retched.

Why was this happening? He had taken his medication?

Faced his fears. Tried his best. It still was not enough. "WHAT IS WRONG WITH ME!" Gary yelled out.

When he exited the elevator on the 19th floor, he needed assistance. He was unable to breathe. His heart was going a hundred miles an hour. He wanted to run and hide but if he did the idea he had of reuniting with Felicity would never happen. He had to get out of Dodge. But this was not a western movie. He reached for his cell. Speed dialled the number his social worker gave him.

Another lonely Friday night.

After preparing herself a nice dinner, she always unwound from the work week snuggling on the sofa, treating herself to a bottle of Chardonnay, binge-watching the series with that hot leading man she dreamed about who was too young for her, kicking down doors to rescue his love or save the world from terrorists armed with stolen nuclear weapons.

Her private line rang.

Her private line hardly rang on weekends.

And never at 1 a.m. Who could that be?

She raced to answer before it went to voice mail or if whoever called didn't leave a message.

She recognised the number on the display.

It was her former client. The lost, ex-soldier.

The cute one from English Canada who had no friends or relatives in Quebec.

He had not left Montreal?

"Jarry? Where are you?"

"At a new job! It's after nine at night! I'm so scared!"

My God, she thought, *he had secured employment again?*

She never encountered him frantic.

He generally was subdued but now in an emotional crisis.

"Deep breaths. In and out, Jarry. You know where you are. Everything is fine," she said in a Quebecois accent.

Assistance from his social worker Ms. Jepson on the phone but his breathing was forced in and out hyperventilating.

"I want to run and hide, but I'll lose everything!"

"Breathe deep, Jarry."

He forced himself to hyperventilate again but gasped.

"It didn't do any good!"

"You on medication?"

"Yes!" Gary yelled back.

If she was there, he could throw himself into her arms.

She snapped out of the reverie.

He was now on 19th floor washroom in a frenzied panic. "I'm a sitting duck!"

Ideas raced through her head.

Was he out of touch with reality or actually experiencing something?

"Who's there?"

"No one—but I can feel it!"

"They're waiting for me," he yelled back.

She was going to have to calmly coach him through this.

"Jarry…"

Gary darted out the washroom.

Grabbed his cart with bucket and mop.

Hit the elevator door button. It immediately popped open.

Two girls in dresses escorted with 2 young men in suits were laughing, obviously intoxicated, beers in their hands.

"Janitor!"

"Jackpot!"

"Superhero?"

English. No French accents. Gary stared at them.

"He doesn't understand?"

"You speak English?"

Gary grunted, still on edge.

"He's got blonde hair!"

"Must be from Germany?"

"We made a mess!"

They continued to laugh and shoot comments at Gary.

"Save our hides?"

"20th floor mess!"

"Beers all over!"

"Clean up, and they're yours."

"Do it!"

"Yea!"

"Pretty please," said the blonde woman in a black dress.

"A-Okay," Gary responded.

They cheered.

The blonde girl blew a kiss. Elevator doors shut.

Appearance of revellers changed thought pattern in his head. Like his thinking went from one channel to another.

"Jarry, who's there?"

"Party animals. They just left."

She heard the sound of a bell.

Gary entered another elevator with mop and bucket.

Doors closing.

"You okay?"

"Yes. Riding up."

His speaking was clear. Has control over his emotions.

"Everything fine now?"

"A-Okay," Gary responded.

"Call me back."

"Will do," Gary answered, clicking off.

She was confounded.

He was not bipolar but on some emotional whirlwind.

She'd wait. See where this went next.

On the 20th floor. No white marble floor to mop up.

It was an event space.

Bar, kitchen, tables, and sofas.

Corporate bash had taken place.

Pizza boxes. Chinese buffet containers. Coffee cups.

Pop Cans and special edition microbrewery beers with goats, reindeers, and joker faces labelling were strewn everywhere.

Gary scooped odds and ends methodically up, loading trash in bags. Wiped counters down and sprayed the room with apple spice air freshener. Grabbed an unopened double six-pack case of 12 beers and left.

As he descended in the elevator towards the basement parkade, he was smiling. He's going to make it.

He's going survive the shift.

He schlepped the 50-pound sack of trash over his shoulder and lugged the case of microbrewery beer towards the container bin. The 20-foot rear gate of the office tower parkade began to rise. His heart almost stopped from shock.

It was as if the bowels of Hades had parted.

The front end of the Mack garbage truck sat idling.

He was a deer frozen in headlights.

The trash truck ready to plow him down.

His shaking hand fumbled to reach for his cell clipped to his belt. He hit the speed dial to his social worker.

It was 30 minutes since she heard from Gary, so she presumed all was fine and returned to binge watching her TV series. Set to speaker phone and she immediately heard his cries.

"No! No! No!"

"Jarry?"

"Garbage men are here!!"

She heard truck engine noise reverberate via her cell.

Reality a fact.

Was Gary's emotional processing and perception of what was transpiring actual or not? she thought.

"Never should have stayed out after 9 o'clock!

I have to quit!"

"Jarry... be strong."

In the cabin, behind the steering, Michel was eyeing the janitor.

"Tabernac," what is his problem.

Shake your head. Your eyes are stuck, clown, he thought.

BLAWWW! Michel leaned on the horn.

The sound made Gary scream.

Ms. Jepson heard it from the speaker phone clearly too.

Gary, transfixed. Petrified frozen.

"I'm stuck," he cried on his cell.

"Have to run and hide before it's too late!"

She had 20 years tenure with the city.

Was respected as a psychiatric social worker by peers.

Now had to do everything in her power to coach him through this demon. If she failed now she failed herself.

"You survived Afghanistan. You will make it," she said.

Horn echoed through the parkade anew.

If he doesn't move in two seconds I'll bounce his butt myself, Michel thought to himself from up in the truck.

"I'll never make it," Gary said into his cell.

"You have to," Ms. Jepson ordered.

Gary stared right in the upper cab at Michel.

Long beard. Shades. A bandana. Disguised so he could kill me and get away clean if any witnesses, Gary thought.

The zombie still didn't move, so Michel jumped out.

He had huge, pumped up muscular biceps and hypertrophied forearms covered with tattoos of dragons, tigers, and skeleton head skulls.

"He's going to throw me into the garbage bin and grind me up," Gary yelled into his cell phone.

She was terrified.

He was on the cusp of breaking down.

"Jarry, trust me."

He was crying now.

"He's coming to get me!"

"Pretend you're in the army. Hold on to the end!"

"How?" Gary cried out.

"Be brave!!"

"I can't!"

Never dated.

Single her whole life.

Tons of love to give and no takers.

If she could channel an iota of that love through the phone to empower Gary, maybe he could prevail.

"Please, Jarry…" she said. "Please…"

It was the most delicate 'please' he ever heard.

Unlike any army order ever.

Gary closed his eyes and waited to be devoured by the garbage man gargoyle.

Instead of shoving, Michel froze.

A 12 sack of beer was by the zombie's feet—he was going to trash it in the bin.

"Tabernac," Michel said French.

Gary opened his eyes.

Garbage man staring at the beer.

"Huh?"

Michel realised the janitor was English.

No wonder, the zombie's not Quebecois…

"The beer? What are you going to do?"

He looked like a killer wrestler but didn't sound nasty?

"What?"

"Them!" Michel pointed to the case of lager.

"The beer?" Gary asked.

"Oui!"

"Nothing. I was going to throw them out."

"Tabernac." *No one wastes beer*, Michel thought.

"Per-Qua?"

Gary didn't understand that. "Huh?"

"Why?" The garbage man reiterated, now again in English.

"I don't drink," Gary answered.

Michel was mystified.

What? he thought, *Impossible?*

"You can have them all if you like," Gary said.

Gary handed the double six pack over.

Michel examined the brand. His face lit up.

"Polish brewskis. Right on, Saigon," Michel uttered in French.

He could tell Gary didn't understand, so Michel backslapped Gary as a gesture for appreciation.

"*Merci beaucoup.* Thanks a zillion, *l'ami*—friend."

"Friend?"

"Oui!"

Gary understood 'oui' meant 'yes' in French.

Impossible, he thought, *he isn't a gargoyle.*

He doesn't want to harm me.

The garbage man stuck out his hand.

Gary gawked at Michel's extended beefy hand.

Then slowly shook it, stunned.

He had a soft grip.

"*Je m'appelle* Michel," he said softly too.

"I'm Gary."

"Jarry," Michel repeated.

Like everyone else in Montreal, the garbage man pronounced his name the same wrong way.

"You work next Friday?"

"Yea," Gary said.

"*Au revoir, sept jours*, Jarry."
"See you then," Gary replied.
Michel jumped back into the garbage truck with his beers.
Gary tossed his bag of trash in the bin.
Prongs dunked bin contents in the belly of the garbage beast on wheels. Compressor squashed it. Michel beeped his horn and exited the parkade.
"Jarry... Jarry?"
She heard voices but didn't know the result?
"You won't believe this. He didn't want to hurt me. I gave him leftover beer I found cleaning. Now he wants to be my pal," Gary told Ms. Jepson ecstatic over his cell.
He did it.
The shift was over.
He survived.

*****

Last time Gary felt a high like this was when his unit shot it out with rebel forces chasing them after a mission, and they were whisked off in a chopper in the sky. Then he realised only part the battle was over.

It was late. 3 a.m. Much later than the 9 o' clock he was ever used to being out and about at.

First part of the battle was won, but the war was not over.

He had to get home, and at this time of night, it was going to be as perilous as being on patrol in the blowing, blinding, dust devils of Afghanistan.

"On my way now. The Metro stopped running so I have to take a bus to Pie-IX Boulevard where I transfer to the last bus of the night to get to my bachelor apartment and be safe," he explained to Ms. Jepson over the cell phone.

He briskly walked along Rene Levesque Boulevard then down Atwater into Little Burgundy. He had been in this neighbourhood before looking for a job at a car wash he didn't get. During the day it was safe, but now drug dealers and addicts congregated about.

He checked the transit app on his phone for the Rue St.

Jacques Bus. 3:15 a.m. He had two minutes. Would have to march faster or reconnoitre a short route on his days off for the future trips.

The bus was on time, and he was able to board quick and avoid 'scary people' loafing on corners. First thing he noticed was a mother. She had bloodshot eyes. Two disheveled children with her were gawking at him.

Gary wondered if they were homeless. As he walked down the aisle, young men in orange and green hoodies with sports team logos had their arms and legs stretched out taking numerous seats.

The bus left downtown and travelled parallel to the St. Lawrence River. Gary could see the silhouette of cranes that loaded goods with huge calipers from foreign freighters docked at the Port of Montreal. An empty bottle rattled and rolled on the floor as the bus pull in and out of stops.

The stench of alcohol permeated and a man in a trench coat lying sideways across seats was snarling to himself in French.

People riding the bus after 9 o 'clock at night were different than the ones who took it during his travels around the city during the day. No old widows lugging grocery bags. Students with knapsacks. Office workers in dresses. Bankers in suits. Passengers thumbing through phones.

The bus came to a stop. Gary glanced out and witnessed a drug deal transaction on a corner. The dealer noticed Gary watching and bashed his fist against the window as the bus pulled away. When Gary glanced forward, he could see the bus driver's eyes staring back in the rear-view mirror.

As the bus continued eastbound, Gary studied the route map on his phone app noting his approaching stop.

"Transfer point. Pie-XI Boulevard," the driver announced in French. Gary dinged the bell. Could see the driver's eyes in the mirror again, following him as he prepared to disembark.

"Merci beaucoup," Gary said, stepping off.

Michel told him this. He was certain it meant thank you.

Good manners and easy to remember in French.

Street people were congregating near the stop where Gary waited for the Pie-IX bus too. They were smoking. Drinking.

Gesticulating and cursing in English and French.

None of them were here when he took this bus route during the day, and they glared over. Gary looked back then away.

"Who's this fucking guy gunning me off?" The dealer, Roddy, said to a Jamaican from T.O. with a flat-top haircut and big fuckin' arms who kept a look out for cops. Roddy had never seen Gary before and shrugged.

The dealer was a Caucasian thug from Hull, 150 miles west, across the river from Canada's capital city Ottawa. He went by the street name 'Stilts' because he liked high top runners and had the rangy frame of an NBA player. Raised English but spoke French which was good for selling weed to Quebecois who didn't use crank or crystal meth. Been dealing on this corner for months and didn't like Gary's baby face.

"Eh, man," Stilts uttered, waltzing up to Gary.

"Hash? Crack? Ganja?"

"No, thank you," Gary politely replied.

Stilts walked off and conferred with Roddy. They chuckled.

It was slow for sales and Stilts was bored. Gary sensed bad vibes from the toughs. Took out his cell. When her phone rang again. She was in bed and assumed it was over. She placed it on speaker.

"Very scary people. Very scary."

Now she overheard voices. Stilts and Roddy were in Gary's personal safety space, and he was backing up.

"S'up, Dude?" Stilts questioned.

"Nothing."

"The fuck you doing around here," Stilts demanded.

"Have to catch the bus home."

"Homie here's got to catch the last bus to his digs," Stilts said. Roddy guffawed. Ms. Jepson overheard the ominous laugh over Jarry's cell. It definitely was not over. He was having an encounter again. This time it truly sounded serious.

"Eh, man. Got a dollar," Roddy demanded.

"Don't have any money," Gary answered.

"What about bus fare?" Stilts ordered.

"I use a Metro Pass."

"Fork over the fucking pass, man," Stilts demanded.

"NO?" Did Stilts and Roddy just hear that?

Gary began backing up away from them.

"I need it to get to my job…" Gary said.

Stilts and Roddy began to move in.

"Please…"

He was in real trouble. Ms. Jepson knew it now too.

"Jarry, where are you…"

Gary glanced at the white signs, but it was too dark to read the black letters and decipher street names.

"I don't know," he replied back frantic.

When they laughed, Gary broke out in a run.

She could hear his footsteps and heavy breathing.

Thugs yelling and threatening Gary to stop.

Ms. Jepson dialled 911.

He knew it. He knew it all along. No matter what all doctors said, it was true. Not a delusion and was happening.

Scary people were after him and chasing him down now.

Never smoking or taking drugs gave him the advantage and he had been in really good shape when he was in the army so was able to get a good start and kept going as they yelled from behind and were tiring out.

Gary cut across streets. Re-traced his path using parked cars as markers to orient himself. Dashed into an alley and ducked behind a minivan. From here he could view the main street and be in proximity to run when the bus arrived.

"Jarry…"

It was his social worker. He adjusted the volume on his phone, so the scary people hunting him wouldn't hear.

"Police are coming. Where are you?"

From the alley, he couldn't decipher the romantic sounding Montreal street sign name. Worse, glanced behind realising he was in a cul-de-sac.

"I'm in a dead-end street," Gary whispered in his phone.

Just when he thought his army escape and evasion training worked, they entered the alley.

"No," Gary whispered to himself.

"Police are on their way…"

Stilts and Roddy heard the social worker's voice over Gary's phone. They shambled over and looked down at Gary cowering behind Van.

"Mon," Roddy said, chuckling.

"This creampuff ain't making it home tonight," Stilts added laughing away.

Zoom—Gary saw his bus fly by. It didn't stop because he wasn't there waiting…

"Emergency! I missed the last bus of the night!"

"Scary people are after me," he cried to his social worker.

"Gimmie that!"

Stilts tore the cell out of Gary's hand.

Clicked it off.

Gary charged, knocking them both aside.

Ran down the alley towards the street.

Stilts and Roddy gave chase.

A cab was going by.

"Over here!" Gary called out.

The cab hit the brakes and stopped. Gary ran over.

Tried to open the rear passenger door but it was locked.

The Cabbie disengaged the lock buttons.

Before Gary could enter, Stilts caught up.

Flicked out a blade and pressed it to Gary's neck.

The cabbie zoomed off.

Stilts held the blade against Gary's jugular.

"Move and you're dead."

Gary whimpered.

Roddy riffled through Gary's pockets.

"Coins. Two bucks change. Cell. Subway Pass…"

Monster sounding engine reverberated through the air.

Stilts and Freddie turned to look for witnesses but the behemoth of a truck or whatever it was passed.

"Game over. You lose, Pip-squeak…"

Just when Stilts thought it was clear to take Gary out a voice in French…

"Tabernac! What ta hell!"

Before Stilts and Roddy could react, it was too late.

Michel, the garbage man, the guy Gary gave the beer to, appears.

"You picking on my friend, uh," Michel said in English. Michel seized the switchblade, slapped Stilts about the face and threw him into a sack of trash.

Roddy charged. Michel kicked him in the stomach.

Roddy doubled over and dropped.

"Shitheads."

Michel scooped up the phone, coins, transit pass, and handed it back to Gary.

"Merci beaucoup."

Michel lifted Stilts up.

Seized him by the throat.

Slammed him against the wall.

"Touch my friend again; you're dead."

Roddy materialized behind, a gun to Michel's head.

Michel froze and raised his arms.

"Think you can mess with us? We own these streets, mon," Stilts gloated at Gary.

"Now, see your friend die, Pip-squeak," Stilts uttered.

Millisecond flash back transported Gary to Afghanistan… Gary races for a helicopter while a firefight transpires.

He can hear screams of his fellowmen via the communication device attached to his helmet.

"Help! I'm alive! I'm alive!" Gary jumped on the helicopter.

"Come back! Save me! Gary!"

Gary ready but hesitates as gun fire intensifies.

"No! Don't leave me hanging!"

Gary watches in horror.

The chopper flies off sideways to the horizon.

We hear screams below. Gary tears down his face.

In that millisecond before Roddy pulls the trigger, Gary springs like a lion, knocking the gun aside as it discharges and misses. Michel decks Roddy across the face, cold-cocking him.

A police car turns, enters the alley.

Stilts runs for it. The cop bolted from his car, ran and tackled Stilts from behind. After they wrestled a few seconds, he restrained Stilts in cuffs.

*****

Michel pulled up to the curb and parked.

Gary was seated on the passenger seat in the truck.

It was now 4:30 a.m. and over for sure now.

"Tabernac, great move."

"Thanks for your help," Gary said.

Gary stepped out of the cab.

"Merci beaucoup for the beer. See you around, Jarry."

Gary waved goodbye.

He began his first night at work fatigued and frightened, but now Gary was so high on adrenaline, he didn't need sleep.

What a night.

Not since the army had he had such a fight.

He had gone to Afghanistan and lost but survived and lived to return home a broken man.

Tonight he went to battle again.

This time survived. Mission accomplished.

He had won and was a new man.

Chapter 18

The following week Genevieve Jepson touched based in an e-mail with a psychiatrist attached to the Canadian Forces of Veteran Affairs in charge of Jarry's case.
She told him of recent developments.

The military psychiatrist further briefed and expanded about his past. Gary had been haunted by delusions of guilt following the death of fellow soldiers in his unit during a black operations mission. When he returned was deemed unfit for duty and after being discharged disappeared. His condition deteriorated as he travelled cross country alone.

An unfortunate personal history began to bedevil him.

How as a baby he was kidnapped by his birth father later killed by Police in a shootout after snatching Gary and concealing him in a garbage bin.

How his cries were heard by emergency responders searching for him, seconds before being crushed into a garbage truck compactor.

How for years, his mother imposed a curfew on Gary to be home by 9 o'clock at night to say his prayers and thank the Lord for interceding before being aborted in a dump.

As a young man unable to abide by her conditions any longer he rebelled. At 24 and unemployed with no prospects, the Canadian Forces was his only way out.

His mother told him she never wanted to see or speak to him again. If he left her, he was as dead as that baby almost crushed in a garbage bin years ago.

He returned home to B.C. to search for his elderly mother ready to listen, behave, obey, and be a good boy again. But she passed a year earlier in a care home which led to his year long, tormented way from Vancouver across the country concluding successfully in Montreal.

The military psychiatrist thanked Ms. Jepson for her intervention. Instead of what could have been a fatal mental breakdown, she was instrumental in saving him.

She dedicated her life to the vulnerable for moments like this. The casualties were far too many. Here an exception. After 20 years, she could count the victories on her fingers. This was why she was called to serve. There was not enough love to go around in this world. It was why so many of the lost ended defeated. Despite that, she and Jarry had won.

Her first new matter after successfully closing his case file was being re-assigned to investigate a case of child abandonment. She interviewed a teacher, a man her age. No wedding band on his left hand. Heavy like her but with a handsome face. And to her surprise, this primary school teacher gentleman asked her out for coffee. And within a week, after all those years, love finally found her.

*****

In the week since being stonewalled by her son Ray, Harry tried contacting hospitals all over Montreal. Half disclosed patient information. Others refused.

He considered regional hospitals, but it was futile since he was not competent enough in French to explain the situational subtleties. His first idea was just to booze it up. How could he live after being graced by her presence and loveliness? His only choice to deal with the withdraw was medicating himself by drinking himself numb.

But, what if he was able to find her?

A big drunk would be disastrous. The other option was his thousand movie collection of DVDs from the good old days. But after all these years and the real-life high of loving May, he doubted the bygone decades of Rock Hudson and Doris Day romance would be a remedy for loneliness.

There had been many empty nights over the years. Wondering where she was, whatever happened to her? May, the one who got away? Now, since meeting her again, he had never felt what he was feeling before. Intoxicated with sensations of hearing, seeing, and holding her in his arms.

The agonizing withdrawal symptoms now. He ached in his bones and soul for her like never before. He had to find her.

He'd be dead in a year if he could not hold her again.

After speaking to Gary on the cell phone one morning, May's condition grew worse. She remained in intensive care, and her situation was now serious.

Her heart rate flux was volatile. A dangerously high blood pressure required a closely monitored cornucopia of medications; there were multiple intravenous's. Hourly blood sampling analysis.

Oxygen for difficulty breathing. Felicity grasped her grandmother's hand and looked in her eyes. Where did she muster such incredible strength? So much braver than herself. Her body shutting down but her grandmother's spirit refusing to submit.

Her ferocious hold and yearning for life made Felicity want to cry. When Felicity retrieved the family cell phone at home in the kitchen cutlery drawer and discovered Gary and Harry's number's blocked, she confronted her daddy.

He denied everything.

"As soon as the show is over I'm moving."

The idea terrified Ray.

"How could you do that to me," he said.

"How could you deprive that sweet, old man of love?"

"What are you talking about?"

Felicity produced the family cell phone.

"You had his number blocked!"

"You're not like your Nanna, Felicity."

"Be smarter and stronger if I was!"

"You're better than her, Felicity."

"Why did you block Gary's number? You know I like him!"

"There are things you don't know about him?"

"About Gary? What could be so bad?"

"Ray showed me a test."
"What kind of test?"
"An aptitude test. He's deficient, Felicity."
"He's not 'deficient', he's wounded," she answered.
"I didn't see bandages or scars on him," Ray responded.
"Exactly—they're invisible," Felicity yelled.
Ray's expression said it better than words.
"It's okay, Daddy. I know you didn't know."
"You're all I'm going to have left, Felicity."
Felicity hugged her daddy.
"Sorry, for being disrespectful."
Ray kissed his baby girl on the forehead.

His mother would have administered a thorough tongue-lashing in this instance. Only his baby girl could forgive so unconditionally. It was just her good nature.

After a few days, the oxygen mask was removed, and May breathed on her own. Two days later her heart was stable.

The following 48 hours May rose out of bed. When Felicity and Ray visited next, she had doffed the hospital smock, was in street clothes, meeting them fully dressed.

Hospital staff found it amusing but didn't know May's character or history. When May announced she was ready to go home with her son and granddaughter, orderlies attempted to detain her, and a physician was called to restore order.

When May walked out on her own two feet again, and he objected she brandished her cane at the good doctor.

The hospital necessitated she sign a disclaimer relieving medical personnel of negligence or responsibility for her actions. Determined she was well enough, May signed her name with triple exclamation marks tagged at the end!

Ray wanted to wheel his mom out but of course, she refused. May exited the doors into the cool and biting crisp, sunny Montreal morning and cheered. She was ready to go home.

Physicians and nurses witnessing it were stunned at her capacity to bounce back after being so close to death. This was who her Grandmother was. She was going to fight, no live on to love another day.

Ray had been on egg shells since Felicity confronted him about shenanigans on the family cell phone to pre-empt Gary and Harry from entering their lives.

When they arrived home and sipped on orange tea, the subject of Gary came up. May wanted to be silent about him resurfacing. Knew Felicity would be crushed if she told her about the last time Gary visited her in the hospital.

"He came to see me before my condition got worse."

Felicity gasped.

"And," Felicity asked.

"He was in trouble and upset."

The words pained Felicity.

"Did he say anything about me?"

"He saw you with Dick. Was worried he lost you?"

"No?"

May dreaded disclosing the rest.

"When you were ill he lost his job and couldn't keep his place."

Felicity began to weep.

A gentle and quiet cry of a little girl.

May took her in her arms. Held her tight.

"You have to let him go."

"Why?" Felicity sobbed.

May took Felicity's face into her palms. Wiped tears.

"Your time is now. Your hard work has paid off."

"Gary and I are meant to be together!"

"You may meet again down the road."

Ray wiped tears running down Felicity's cheeks.

"What day is it today?"

"Thursday, you're off, remember?" Ray added.

Thursday, Felicity thought.

She recollected what Gary ate that day.

"Nanna?"

"Yes?"

"I need to borrow the car?"

They felt best to not ask why.

Ray handed over the keys no questions asked.

Chapter 19

Gary attempted to ring May again with no luck so assumed Ray discovered he visited her in the hospital and re-blocked his number again. He didn't have a chance to pop by since he had the janitor job now and was working late evenings combined with taking the medication that caused him to sleep into afternoons.

After surviving the 1st night in the dudgeon of doom, he still got jitters returning but it turned into a high-five high each night after he completed an 8-hour shift.

Bill asked if he could work a 7-day stretch and Gary accepted profusely. When Gary explained the problem concerning the loss of his place Bill advanced him two weeks' pay which enabled him to keep his cosy apartment with the beautiful view of the downtown buildings in the distance.

At 14.98 an hour with extra money left, Gary stocked his kitchen with tuna fish, pasta, and more expensive lean ground beef meat for spaghetti Saturdays. He also picked up a rib-eye steak to sizzle with HP sauce and extra creamery chocolate fudge ice cream as extra treats.

Lastly, Bubble Gum. Jujubes. Jawbreakers and Gummy bears. He got a sweet high from a confectionery candy but it didn't make up for not having Felicity to hug.

He worked 7 days straight and was off. A new sense of calm about his bearing. It was a time to celebrate. There was no pressure any more.

No worry about being careful how much money to have till the end of the month. Gary now had expendable income and went out to treat himself.

The place was down the street from the Guy Metro station. Felicity mentioned and he passed often since moving to Montreal and overheard English students on the Metro talk about it being the best chicken joint in town.

Inside the restaurant teemed with multitudes of customers. Friends, families, lovers. Gary was the only solo person present. Some Montrealers found that strange and started wondering who was that lone individual feasting with such joie de vivre. Gary was not self-conscious and enjoyed the rotisserie chicken he was devouring.

First, she drove to his place, knocked on the door and discovered he wasn't home. She found him just where he said he would be if he could one day afford it on Thursdays or on 'soul food day'. The Bar-B-Barn on Guy Street.

Felicity stood in the alcove as Gary licked house sauce off his fingers polishing spare ribs ordered post-fire oven rotisserie chicken. He saw Felicity and stopped chewing, frozen.

A bored Gentleman out with his wife watching the loner gorging with gusto then freezing mid-meal caused him to burst laughing. His wife followed her husband's train of sight and asked him in French what the joke was?

Felicity was grinning too.

Gary wanted to dart over and sweep her in his arms.

But the incident with Dick at the sports bar caused him to tentatively stand there, so Felicity walked up to the table.

"Hi," Felicity said softly.

"Hi," Gary answered.

"Soul food day today?"

"Yes. You remembered?"

"Yes," she answered.

What was she doing here?

This was a good thing.

He was delighted to see her, and his heart began to race.

"Spare ribs too, huh," she added.

"Yes," hardly able to answer.

"Like to help me eat them up?"

Felicity got a kick munching on Texas-style ribs from a metal bucket. Even eating, she was so amazing. Just the way she conducted herself. So comfortable and at ease.

She is so wonderful.
Could he ever hold her again?
He doubted it.
She was everything he was not.
Even with his new job and not being on welfare anymore, he did not have the elegance and poise she possessed training in ballet so many years and being as beautiful as she was.
Felicity could feel something wrong.
"What is it?"
"May I ask you a question?"
"Sure?"
"Where is your new boyfriend?"
She had to handle this carefully.
"He put our relationship to the test."
"What do you mean by that?"
"Tried to help me overcome a fear."
"Did it work?"
"It only made things worse."
"Sorry to hear that."
"That's okay. I felt his method was crude."
That was the last of the ribs.
She wiped her lips with a napkin.
Gary as well. She laughed.
"What?" he asked.
"Got goo on your lip."
Gary wiped his mouth again. It was still on his face.
"Hold on a second."
Felicity reached over and wiped it off.
"You missed a spot."
"Thanks," he said.
She smiled.
"Felicity?"
"Yes?"
"You know something?"
"What?"
"I know something Dick and the doctors don't know."
"What?"
"You're…"

"What?"
"Just delicate."
"Delicate?"
"Yes, extra delicate. And I like you that way."
They were looking at each other.
Both wondering the same thing.
Could it still happen?
"I called you a few times after 9 o'clock, but there was no answer," she said.
"I found a new job."
"You work after 9 at night!"
"Yes. I'm here to celebrate."
"You must be very brave."
"I had to be. To pay my rent. Be off welfare.
Stay in Montreal…"
He hesitated "…be with you."
She gasped. Her hair, teeth, and skin.
But the sum of Felicity was more than obvious physical attributes. Gary loved something guys didn't seem to see…
A softness about her bearing—her super soft heart.
To Gary, it made Felicity as beautiful as a full super moon.
"Would you like dessert?" he asked.
"It's not the end of the month," she said, grinning.
"Every weekend is the Sweetest Day now."
They fed each other upside down pineapple cake with walnuts topped with a cherry on top the way Gary suggested her they do on the Sweetest Day.
Relishing the taste on their palate, slowly swishing it around their mouths as long as possible before swallowing, savouring it on end. All the while, looking into each other's eyes to make the sweet simplicity last.
When they left and were on the sidewalk, it was the moment of truth. Their impromptu 2nd Sweetest Day dessert date was over. The recent hospitalisation had still affected and somewhat rattled her. Gary was tense because the bliss of being with Felicity again was coming to an end.

Felicity possessed the savoir fare and awareness to realise his uneasiness and her winning smile disarmed him. They stopped.

"I have something to tell you?"

"Yes?" she said, looking closely at him.

He had prevailed over the dudgeon of doom.

Allied himself with the garbage men gargoyles.

He just had one final brave act to perform.

Now. Gary. Please. Make your move, she thought.

Gary took her hand, saving the night.

"I am so in love with you."

They kissed. Feelings flowing through them amazing.

Something he had never had. He had found her again. Felicity would be all he needed. Comfort and peace. Her softness to feel the aching void. She felt his heart beating so fast right through the muscles he got from army training through her sweater and loved this about Gary.

She couldn't wait to get to know him. No man had ever reacted to her like this. The sweetness of it completely enchanted and overtook her. How could she ever want to destroy herself? So close, so close to losing it all.

She never would have found him if she did.

Thank God she failed.

She was never going to let Mr. Perfect go again.

*****

The idea was for May to host a dinner over the Christmas—New Year's holidays for Ray and Harry as well as the two new lovebirds Felicity and Gary. This gave her time to also prepare herself to welcome Harry back into her life and see where wings of love would carry them.

Christmas carols blaring on the car radio.

Crowded department stores. Holiday gift hunting hype. Supermarket searching for the biggest turkey so Ray could have leftover sandwiches for work. Teaming Jean Talon Market sifting for vegetables and fresh quality spuds so Harry could enjoy mashed potatoes.

Apples in season for fresh baked pie.

As the dinner approached, emotions disrupted her weaker body, and she was overwhelmed. May was so stressed the experience induced heart palpitations and Ray returned her to the hospital. Luckily, a physician diagnosed it as anxiety and recommended she just relax, so they cancelled the dinner.

In the end, she invited Harry over solo for him and her to spend New Year's Day together. Not seeing or hearing from May in a month left him to assume the worse. He supposed Ray convinced her that interloper was best walked away from for the family's benefit. But May called. Lady Luck late in life had not left. The reality was she was incommunicado from being hospitalized due to her heart.

Harry showed up on her door in his trademark black and white suit, dry-cleaned and pressed. Expensive cologne purchased on St. Catherine Street. Spiff and polished shiny shoes. Trench coat. Scarf, minus the fedora in favour of the healthy head of neatly combed back hair giving him the appearance being years younger.

"Ray says we are wrong for each other, Harry."

"The only important thing is how we feel," he said

They spoke of old days in Montreal.

Good times and bad.

People known now gone and passed on.

"I'm not long for this world either," she told him.

"Time to bring the old-time magic back again," he said.

It was sunny.

Then turned a balmy 10 Celsius above.

Families in the neighbourhood were about strolling by.

They decided to relish the moment.

Visit Mont Royal Park for a stroll.

On a bench in the company of young lovers, Harry took her. What joy she felt. The life force in his hug rejuvenated her instantly. So many men during her long storied love life.

She had never experienced a man relate to her his way before. Searching and never really finding the right fit.

Harry. The innocence in him real.

The twinkle in his eyes.

How he touched her.

86 years old as if she was an innocent 20.

A sensation unlike anything ever experienced in her heart.

She was gold. A diamond in his arms.

A bird was chirping in an oak tree above.

Harry recognised the sparrow's distinct tweet.

Taken photos of it. Recognised the spotted plumage.

The sparrow following him around during what was going to be the last year of wandering around the park in his lonely life.

Harry cupped May's face. The wait finally over.

So much time. All the passing seasons wondering.

Afflicted by loneliness, yet blessed with physical health to endure. After so long, finally able to savour the simple sweetness of May in his arms. The sparrow continued to chirp. *Great life, great, great life*, he reflected.

THE END